PRAISE FOR
BIG FOOT AND LITTLE FOOT

"VERDICT: Established chapter book author
Potter delivers another winner."
—*School Library Journal*

"A charming friendship story." —*Kirkus Reviews*

"A fun romp with valuable lessons in
friendship and forgiveness." —*Booklist*

BIG F🦶🦶T
and LITTLE F🦶🦶T

BOOK 2

THE MONSTER DETECTOR

Story by Ellen Potter

Art by Felicita Sala

AMULET BOOKS

NEW YORK

For Elias and Ilan

The Library of Congress has cataloged the hardcover edition as follows:
Names: Potter, Ellen, 1963- author. | Sala, Felicita, illustrator.
Title: The Monster Detector / by Ellen Potter ; illustrated by Felicita Sala.
Description: New York: Amulet Books, 2018. | Series: Big foot and little foot; Book 2 | Summary:
Hugo, a young sasquatch, and his friend Gigi use a Monster Detector to find a Green Whistler,
but when Hugo's human friend, Boone, joins in, surprises are in store.
Identifiers: LCCN 2018001832 | ISBN 978-1-4197-3122-8 (hardcover pob)
Subjects: | CYAC: Yeti—Fiction. | Monsters—Fiction. | Schools—Fiction. | Friendship—
Fiction.
Classification: LCC PZ7.P8518 Mo 2018 | DDC [E]—dc23

Paperback ISBN 978-1-4197-3386-4

Text copyright © 2018 Ellen Potter
Illustrations copyright © 2018 Felicita Sala
Book design by Siobhán Gallagher

Printed and bound in U.S.A.
10 9 8 7 6 5 4 3 2 1

Amulet Books are available at special discounts when purchased in quantity for premiums and
promotions as well as fundraising or educational use. Special editions can also be created to
specification. For details, contact specialsales@abramsbooks.com or the address below.

Amulet Books® is a registered trademark of Harry N. Abrams, Inc.

ABRAMS The Art of Books
195 Broadway, New York, NY 10007
abramsbooks.com

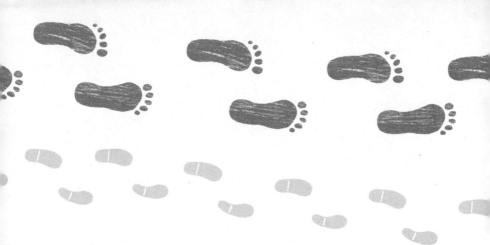

The Big Foot and Little Foot series

Book One: *Big Foot and Little Foot*

Book Two: *The Monster Detector*

Book Three: *The Squatchicorns*

1

Monster in a Box

Deep in the cold North Woods, there lived a young Sasquatch named Hugo. He was bigger than you but smaller than me, and he was hairier than both of us. He lived in apartment 1G in the very back of Widdershins Cavern with his mother and father and his older sister, Winnie.

It was Saturday, which was the day that mail was delivered to Widdershins Cavern. Hugo stood at the end of the long line at the post office, waiting to see if his package had arrived. Every so often he would jump up as high as he could.

"What are you doing, Hugo?" asked a voice behind him. It was his friend Gigi. She was on the small side for a squidge (which is what you call a young Sasquatch) but she had excellent posture, which made her look a little taller. She was holding a letter.

"I'm waiting in line," he answered.

"No, I mean, why are you jumping up and down?" Gigi asked.

"I'm trying to see if there's a large package on the post office shelf," Hugo replied.

"If there is, it might be mine." He jumped up again, but he couldn't see over the heads of all the grown-up Sasquatches in front of him.

"What's in the package?" Gigi asked.

"I'm not sure," he answered. "It's from Mad Marvin."

"Mad Marvin? You mean the guy who makes Mad Marvin's Monster Cards?"

Hugo nodded. "If you collect one hundred wrappers from Mad Marvin's Monster Cards and mail them in, Mad Marvin will send you a special prize. I mailed mine in last week. I've been collecting them for three years. No one in all of Widdershins Cavern has ever collected that many wrappers."

Gigi crossed her arms over her chest and stared hard at Hugo. "You think Mad Marvin is sending you a monster, don't you, Hugo?"

"No," Hugo answered quickly. But after a moment, he admitted, "Well, maybe." Suddenly he had an idea. "Hey, Gigi, if you climb up on my shoulders, you'll be able to see if there's a large package on the shelf." Then he remembered that Gigi was sensitive about being small, so he added, "I mean, I *would* climb on *your* shoulders, but you have better balance than I do."

Gigi thought about this for a second. A special prize was always interesting, even if it wasn't a monster.

"Okay," she said. "Hold this." She handed her letter to Hugo.

He knelt down and Gigi climbed onto his shoulders. Slowly, he stood up while she gripped the long hair on his neck.

"Do you see anything?" he asked after a moment.

"I see Mrs. Rattlebags," Gigi said. "She's

at the counter, complaining about some-thing."

"That's nothing new," said Hugo. Mrs. Rattlebags was always complaining about something.

"But do you see a package?" he asked impatiently.

"Yep," said Gigi. "And it's so big they couldn't even put it on the shelf. They put it on the floor instead."

"How big is it?" Hugo asked excitedly.

Gigi considered. "You could fit a squidge in it," she said.

A squidge . . . *or a monster*, thought Hugo.

"And it's in a wooden crate," Gigi contin-ued. "Wait, there are words written on the

crate. The first word is . . . CAUTION!"

CAUTION! That was a good sign, thought Hugo. If you were going to mail a monster, you would definitely write CAUTION! on the crate.

"What else does it say?" Hugo asked.

Gigi wiggled around on his shoulders, then said, "I can't see. Can you stand on your tiptoes?"

Hugo stood on his tiptoes.

"Higher," she said.

He stood on the very tip of his tiptoes.

"It says LIVE CARGO!," Gigi told him.

"LIVE CARGO! Then there is a monster in

there!" he cried. Hugo got so excited that he forgot to keep still. Gigi bobbled around on his shoulders, then slid down his back in a very undignified way. She fell on the ground, backside first.

"Sorry," Hugo said as he helped her to her feet.

After *harrumphing* with annoyance, Gigi patted down the three thin braids on the side of her head and stood up even straighter than before.

"I told you!" Hugo said. "Mad Marvin *did* send a monster! I wonder which one it is. It could be a Shivering Wisp. Or a Black-Toed Oozer . . . no, that's bigger than two squidges. Maybe it's a Six-Headed Screecher."

"Hugo, monsters aren't real," Gigi said.

"Of course they're real. For instance, I always thought Humans were a kind of monster, until I met Boone." Boone was Hugo's best friend, a Human boy who lived on the banks of Ripple Worm River. "And Boone thought Sasquatches were monsters until he met us. A monster is just a creature you've never seen before and are a little afraid of. But when you meet it, it's just sort of . . . regular. But better."

Gigi thought about that for a second. She was an excellent thinker, and in the end she had to admit that made perfect sense.

2

Mad Marvin's Special Prize

As the line inched forward, Hugo could hardly stand the suspense. He wondered what his mother would say about the monster. If it was a Shivering Wisp, she might think it was cute. Still, Hugo would prefer a Six-Headed Screecher. He wondered if you had to feed all six of the heads.

Hugo couldn't wait to show the monster to Boone. Boone knew all about monsters. He and Hugo were going to become cryptozoologists when they grew up. (A cryptozoologist is a hard-to-say word for someone who studies mysterious creatures.) Now Hugo and Boone would have a real, live monster to take care of!

Finally, Hugo and Gigi reached the post office counter.

"Hi, Mr. Kipper!" Hugo said to the postmaster as he bounced up and down with anticipation.

"Well, good morning, Hugo. You look like someone who is expecting a package today."

Hugo nodded and looked at the crate on the floor.

"Well, I might just have something with your name on it." Mr. Kipper winked. Then he turned around, but instead of lifting up the crate, he went to the shelf and picked up a little square package.

"Here you go." Mr. Kipper handed Hugo the little package. Hugo's name and address were written on it, and Mad Marvin's name was written above the return address. The package was so small it fit in the palm of Hugo's hand. It did not say WARNING or LIVE CARGO on the package. Instead, it said FRAGILE.

That meant whatever was inside it could be broken.

And since monsters cannot be broken, it also meant that there was no monster inside.

"Is there anything else for me?" Hugo asked Mr. Kipper in a small but hopeful voice, still eyeballing the large crate.

"No, I'm afraid that's it."

"Oh. Well . . . thanks," Hugo said.

Hugo waited while Gigi mailed her letter, and the two of them walked out of the post office.

"Well? Aren't you going to open your package?" Gigi asked him.

Hugo shrugged. "I guess so."

It was hard to get excited about something that wasn't a monster.

Hugo tore open the package, pulled out a little wooden box, and removed the lid. Both he and Gigi stared down at what was inside.

"Hmm," said Gigi.

"Hmm," said Hugo.

It was a little square piece of wood. In the middle of the square was a round glass window with five white specks inside.

"What do you think it is?" Hugo asked.

"It looks like a compass. Sort of."

Hugo took it out of its box. There was a black strap attached to it.

"It's not a compass, it's a watch!" said Hugo excitedly. He'd never owned a watch before.

"I don't think it's a watch, either," said Gigi. "Wait. There's a note in the box."

She pulled out the note and unfolded it. This is what it said:

Congratulations! You are now the proud owner of a genuine Monster Detector! Inside your detector are five weechie-weechie moths. When a monster is nearby, they will make a clicking sound by flapping their wings.

We have included a bag of weechie-weechie food. Open the lid on the back of the detector and drop in a pinch each week, along with a drop of water.

Here are a few of the monsters you might find with your Monster Detector:

Red-Nosed Gruzzles, Thorny Wrigglers, Pink-Eyed Pookas, and Hairless Wolly-Wollys.

Good luck finding monsters!

Sincerely,

Mad Marvin

"Wow!" Hugo said, examining the Monster Detector.

"What's a Hairless Wolly-Wolly?" Gigi asked.

It wasn't often that Gigi asked Hugo a question. Gigi usually knew everything about everything. But Hugo did know more about monsters than she did.

"Let's see, a Hairless Wolly-Wolly . . ."

Hugo looked up at the cavern's ceiling, then down at his hairy feet, and then back at Gigi. "It's about the size of a raccoon . . . and it has a scrunched-up

kind of face with long, pointy ears . . . and
. . . it has no hair."

He wasn't absolutely sure about this,
except for the "no hair" part.

"Oh." Gigi nodded. "Sounds weird."

"Well, it *is* a monster, after all."

"Until you meet it," Gigi said. "Then it's
sort of regular."

"Regular . . . but better," Hugo reminded
her.

3

The Monster Search

Y ou know what we should do now?" Hugo said, strapping the Monster Detector on his wrist.

"Look for monsters?" Gigi guessed.

Hugo nodded.

"But how are we going to look for monsters if we can't go outside?" Gigi asked.

Squidges were only allowed to go outside the cavern once in a while, with their school and on special holidays. Although the Big Wide World was an exciting place, it was also dangerous for Sasquatches. There were all sorts of stories about Humans who hunted Sasquatches. Sometimes the Humans wanted to capture them and put them in a cage to study them. Sasquatches needed practice and skill to stay safe in the Big Wide World.

"We can look for monsters right here, in the cavern," suggested Hugo. "There might be one or two."

Gigi gave him a doubtful look.

"Maybe really small ones," he said.

They started their monster search by

traveling down to the east end of the cavern. But it was all apartments down on that end, with lots of Sasquatches going to and fro. It didn't seem like the sort of place a monster would be.

They turned around and headed to the west end of the cavern instead. It was quieter there. There were no apartments and no Sasquatches. They ambled along slowly while Hugo held out his wrist with the Monster Detector on it, and they listened for a *click-click* sound.

The cavern looked different here. The path was narrower. The rock walls were lumpy and had rusty orange lines swirling through them. Hugo and Gigi walked and walked, but the Monster Detector had not made a single sound.

"Maybe it's broken," said Hugo, stopping to tap on the detector's glass window.

"Or maybe there just aren't any monsters around here," Gigi said.

Click-click.

"Did you hear that?" Hugo whispered.

Gigi nodded.

Click-click. Click-click.

They looked at the Monster Detector. In the little glass window, the weechie-weechie moths were flapping their tiny wings.

Click-click! Click-click!

"There must be a monster here!" Hugo whispered.

They checked all around them, but they didn't see anything suspicious.

"Wait, look at that," Gigi said suddenly, pointing up.

There was an opening at the top of the wall where a thin sliver of light peeped through. Hugo held the Monster Detector up toward it.

CLICK-CLICK-CLICK-CLICK-CLICK!!!! went the weechie-weechie moths.

"The monster must be on the other side of the wall," whispered Gigi.

They both looked up at the opening at the top of the wall. It was high above the ground.

"I could climb up there and have a look," Hugo said.

He was pretty sure Gigi would tell him that that was a stupid idea. She would tell him that it was too dangerous.

But instead Gigi said, "It's the only way to find out."

"Right," he said.

He didn't move.

"I can't think of any other way," he said.

He still didn't move.

"Can you?" he asked.

"I'll do it if you don't want to," Gigi offered.

So of course Hugo had to say that he *did* want to.

He took a deep breath. Carefully, he placed his foot in a little hollow in the wall. He found a shallow ledge on which to place his hand. Slowly, he began to climb. His foot slipped once and he scrambled to find another ledge.

"Are you all right?" Gigi called up.

"I'm totally fine," he said.

Which was not really true. He was barely even mostly fine.

The higher he climbed, the more frantically the weechie-weechie moths *click-clicked*.

"*Shhh!*" he whispered to them.

Finally, Hugo gripped the edge of the hole in the wall. With all his strength, he pulled himself up and peered through the gap. His eyes grew wide. His mouth fell open.

"What?! What do you see?" Gigi whispered.

"Whoa!" was all Hugo could manage to say.

4

The Green Whistler

On the other side of the wall was a small room, no bigger than your bedroom closet. One of the walls in the room had an opening that led out to the Big Wide World. It was large enough for a full-grown Sasquatch to walk through, if they ducked their head a little. Scattered on the ground in the room were

clumps of dark green fur. In one corner
there was a pile of small bones.

"Something lives here, Gigi," Hugo
whispered down to her.

"A Sasquatch?" Gigi whispered back.

Hugo shook his head. "There are bones.
Sasquatches don't eat meat."

"Maybe a bear?" Gigi suggested.

"Have you ever heard of a bear with
green fur?" Hugo asked.

"Green fur?" Suddenly Gigi looked alarmed. "It must be the Green Whistler!"

Hugo felt his foot begin to slip, and he came back down to the ground in a sliding, skidding, bumping way.

"The Green Whatsit?" he asked as he checked his feet for scrapes.

"The Green *Whistler*! My grandmother told me about it. It was this horrible creature that used to live in Widdershins Cavern. They called it the Green Whistler because it was covered in green fur, and right before it pounced on its victims it made this weird whistling noise."

"Really?"

"Really. And my grandmother said there was a rumor that it ate squidges."

Hugo and Gigi stared at each other in the darkness. The only sound was the *click-click-click* of the Monster Detector.

"Um, I'd better get going," said Hugo. "I think my parents wanted me to help at the store."

"Yeah, I think I still have some homework to do," Gigi said.

Then Hugo and Gigi turned around and walked back the way they had come. But this time they walked *a lot* faster.

5

Snarfles

Hugo's family owned the Every-thing-You-Need General Store and Bakery. On Saturday morning the store was always busy. Today, all the little round tables were filled with customers eating blackberry snarfles, which are sort of like waffles except they are shaped like oak leaves.

Other customers were examining items on the store's shelves, like jugs of shampoo (most Sasquatches go through a dozen jugs of shampoo a month), and hacksaws and jigsaws and crosscut saws, because all Sasquatches are experts when it comes to making things out of wood. There were also colorful scarves for fashionable Sasquatches and diapers for baby Sasquatches, and high up on a shelf was a Human Repellent, which smelled just like skunk when you sprayed it. That

was for when you were walking in the woods and wanted Humans to stay away.

Hugo's mom was behind the counter, ringing up purchases. When she saw Hugo, she smiled and waved.

"Hugo!" she called to him over the customers' heads. "Can you run back to the kitchen and ask Grandpa to make some more mushroom tarts? We're all out!"

"Sure, Mom!" Hugo called back.

He started toward the kitchen, passing the little dining room where his sister,

Winnie, was working. She was wiping down a table with a wet rag very slowly while talking to two big Sasquatch boys sitting at the next table. Her lips were an alarming shade of purple and very shiny. She had slathered them with the huckleberry lip gloss that she made herself.

She stopped talking to the boys long enough to notice Hugo.

"What is that ridiculous thing on your wrist?" she asked him.

"It's a Monster Detector," Hugo replied.

"A Monster Detector!? *HA!*" Winnie blurted out, and the big Sasquatch boys looked at each other and smirked.

"*HA*, yourself! It actually works," Hugo

told her. "The bugs inside of it flap their wings and make a clicking sound whenever a monster is close by."

Winnie snorted. "Good thing it's not a Weirdo Detector or it would click whenever *you* got near it."

The Sasquatch boys laughed at that, and Winnie smiled at them.

Hugo held his wrist out toward Winnie and waved it around her head for a moment. "Well, I guess we know it's not a Big Flirt Detector," he said. "If it was, the bugs would be flapping so hard right now that their wings would fall off!"

Winnie's face turned a deep pink. She raised her arm with the dirty rag in it and chucked it at Hugo's head. He ducked just

in time, then made a quick dash for the kitchen.

Grandpa was pouring batter into the snarfle iron. The counter was lined with plates, waiting for more snarfles to be piled on top of them.

"Hi, Grandpa," Hugo said. "Mom says we need more mushroom tarts."

"More? But I made a dozen this morning! Phew, it's been busy today! Why don't you handle the snarfle iron while I make more tarts?"

"Sure!"

Hugo loved using the snarfle iron. He could make a perfect leaf-shaped snarfle almost as well as Grandpa.

Grandpa fired up the oven and opened the kitchen's back door so that the room wouldn't get too hot and smoky. Baking in a cavern could be tricky.

While Grandpa sliced mushrooms for the tarts, Hugo poured snarfle batter onto the hot snarfle iron.

"Grandpa," Hugo said, "do you know anything about the Green Whistler?"

Grandpa looked startled. "The Green Whistler! Well, well, well. I haven't heard that name since I was a little squidge. Why do you ask?"

"Because I think I saw it. Or at least, I

saw where it lives." Hugo described how he and Gigi found the little room at the west end of the cavern and how he had climbed to the top of the wall to peek in. "There were bones and green fur and everything."

Grandpa frowned. "You and Gigi shouldn't have been wandering around the cavern like that, Hugo."

"I know. But Grandpa, did the Green Whistler really eat squidges?"

There was no answer. Grandpa seemed deep in thought. Hugo repeated his question.

"Oh, no, no," Grandpa answered, "that was just a lot of silly talk."

But there was no doubt about it . . . Grandpa looked worried.

6

The Academy for Curious Squidges

Before school started on Monday, all the squidges gathered around Hugo to look at his Monster Detector.

"Doth ip erk?" asked Izzy.

Izzy wore headgear for his overbite, so he spoke a little funny. Fortunately, Hugo almost always understood him.

"Of course it works!" Hugo said. "In

fact, it's already found a monster." He told them about the Green Whistler, and when they didn't believe him, Gigi said it was all true, every word of it.

Just then, Mrs. Nukluk entered the classroom. They all rushed over to their desks and sat down. As usual, Mrs. Nukluk was wearing her long white cloak made of goose feathers.

"Good morning, class," she said. "We've got a busy day ahead of us, and later this morning I have a big surprise for you!"

The squidges looked at each other excitedly.

"Maybe it's a microscope," Gigi whispered to Hugo.

Hugo hoped it was something more fun than a microscope, but he didn't say that to Gigi.

"Does the surprise explode?" asked Malcolm.

"No, it does not, and please raise your hand if you have something to say."

Malcolm raised his hand. "Are you going to pull an egg out of your nose?"

"Why on *earth* would I do that, Malcolm?"

"Because you said there was going to be a big surprise. And that would be very surprising."

Mrs. Nukluk took a deep breath. Deep

breaths seemed to help her when she spoke to Malcolm.

"Take out your math books, everyone. We'll start right in on measurements—"

At that moment a small Human boy walked into the classroom. He had thirty-eight freckles and he carried a paper bag.

"Boone!" cried Hugo.

You weren't supposed to shout in class, but Hugo was so shocked to see his friend that he couldn't help himself.

"Is Boone the surprise, Mrs. Nukluk?" asked Pip.

"No," said Mrs. Nukluk, "but I must admit I *am* surprised. What are you doing here, Boone?"

"I've been thinking about it, and I've

finally decided—" said Boone, smiling at them all. "I want to go to squidge school!"

7

Snuds and Stonkers

Mrs. Nukluk looked confused.

"Don't you have your own school? A *Human* school?" she asked.

"I'm homeschooled. But my grandmother said that if a school opened up in the North Woods, I could go to it. And now that I know about the Academy for

Curious Squidges, I've decided I want to go."

"Well . . . well . . . we've never had a Human in our school. I'm not sure if it's . . ." Mrs. Nukluk searched for the right word.

"Please, Mrs. Nukluk, *please* let Boone join our school!" cried Hugo.

Mrs. Nukluk was so flustered that she forgot to remind Hugo to raise his hand.

"I know all my state capitals," Boone said to her. "And I can spell pretty good, except I get my *f*'s and *ph*'s mixed up sometimes. Plus, I brought my own lunch." He held up his bag.

Mrs. Nukluk considered. "Well, I suppose you can spend the day here. After that, we'll just have to see. There's an empty seat next to Roderick. You can sit there for now."

Roderick Rattlebags's hand shot up in the air.

"Yes, Roderick?"

"I refuse to sit next to a Human," Roderick said in a puffed-up way.

Boone had been walking happily over to Roderick's desk, but now he stopped short. His smile disappeared.

"Boone is just as good as any squidge!" Gigi snapped at Roderick.

"And better than some!" Hugo added, glaring at Roderick.

"Our school is called the Academy for Curious *Squidges*," Roderick shot back at them in a spiteful way, "not Curious *Humans*."

"That's enough," Mrs. Nukluk said. "Please sit down, Boone." Then she turned a stern face to Roderick. "You will share your math book with Boone."

Roderick made a disgusted huffing noise while Boone sat down next to him. The desk and chair were made for squidges, who are much larger than Human children. Boone's head barely peeped over the desk, and his legs dangled off the ground. Roderick looked down at him with a sneer and shifted his chair as far away from Boone as possible.

Mrs. Nukluk led the class through a review of what they had been learning the past week in math. It was all easy stuff, like how many shucklings were in a snud.

Boone raised his hand.

"Yes, Boone?" said Mrs. Nukluk.

"What's a snud?" he asked.

The whole class turned to stare at him, flabbergasted. Even the smallest squidges knew what a snud was!

"It's a unit of measurement," said Mrs. Nukluk. "It's about half the size of a stonker."

"A what?" asked Boone.

Hugo frowned. What was Boone's grandmother teaching him if he didn't even know what a snud or a stonker were?

Mrs. Nukluk opened up her desk drawer and took out her measuring stick. It was a straight piece of maple branch with marks burned into it.

"You see, Boone," she said patiently, placing one finger about halfway up the stick, "this much is a snud."

Boone squinted at the stick for a moment. Then

he smiled his big smile. "*Ohhh!* I get it! A snud is a foot!"

"Excuse me?" Mrs. Nukluk looked confused.

"A snud is a foot," Boone repeated.

"A snud is a *snud*," Mrs. Nukluk said firmly.

"Which is also a foot," insisted Boone.

Now, you and I both know that Boone meant a "foot" in the measuring sort of way, such as "there are twelve inches in a foot." But Sasquatches don't know about feet and yards and inches. That's why Mrs. Nukluk's face suddenly grew very irritated.

"A snud is *not* a foot," she told Boone sternly. "It's not a hand nor an earlobe nor a tongue either. And if you are going to be in this classroom, you'll have to behave and not act so silly."

Boone turned bright red. He slumped in his seat while Roderick smirked at him.

Things had not gotten off to a good start.

8

X-treme Creepy Cryptids

After math, everyone carved little owls out of stumps in woodshop. I know that sounds like fun—and it is—but for Sasquatches, woodworking is very serious business. Sasquatches make nearly everything out of wood, so even the littlest squidges have to learn to do it well.

Luckily, Boone had already done lots of wood carving. Before long he had carved an owl that was just as nice as any of the squidges', and Mrs. Nukluk said so, too.

After woodworking came recess. Everyone bolted out of their chairs to play the Ha-Ha Game or Frog King, which involves a lot of hopping and clapping and kicking, and someone almost always winds up getting hurt, but only just a little.

Hugo hurried over to Boone, who was sliding off his squidge-sized chair.

"I brought something to show you," Boone said, reaching into his back pocket. He pulled out a thick stack of cards with a rubber band around them. The cards had colorful pictures of strange creatures on them.

"What is that?" Hugo asked as he eagerly watched Boone take off the rubber band.

"They're called X-treme Creepy Cryptids cards," Boone told him.

Izzy and Malcolm, who were playing Frog King nearby, overheard and ran over to look.

"What are cryptids?" asked Malcolm.

"Well, they're sort of like monsters," said Boone.

"Wow! So these are Monster Cards for *Humans*!" Malcolm said this so loud that it brought the rest of the class over, too. Even Roderick sauntered over, peering at the cards while pretending not to be interested.

Boone gave each squidge a small stack to look at. On one side there was a colorful picture of a cryptid, and on the other side there was information about it. The monsters on the X-treme Creepy Cryptids cards were different from the monsters on Mad Marvin's cards. On Boone's cards there was a chupacabra, and the Jersey Devil, and a Goatman, which had a Human body and the head of a goat with horns. There were mermaids and mermen, and a sewer alligator. There was even a card for an Ogopogo, a creature that Hugo and Boone had once spotted on the Ripple Worm River.

Hugo was so happy that Boone was making friends, he had to bite his lip to keep from smiling the whole time.

The squidges read all about the cryptids on the backs of the cards. But Boone also told them extra things about the cryptids that weren't even on the cards.

"How do you know all this stuff?" Malcolm asked Boone.

"Because I'm going to be a cryptozoologist one day," Boone told him. "So is Hugo. We have to know all about cryptids."

"Why? So you can capture them?" asked Malcolm.

"No, so we can *understand* them. A cryptozoologist is sort of like a cryptid's best friend."

"*Eww*, look at this thing!" said Pip, holding up a card showing a huge, creepy-looking beast. Its mouth was open as though it were roaring, showing long, sharp fangs dripping with gooey saliva. Its angry eyes were red and squinty. It was covered with tangled hair, and it held up a club as though it were about to thwack it down on someone's head.

"Can I see that?" asked Gigi. Pip handed her the card, and Gigi read from the back:

SASQUATCH

∞∞∞

Also known as Bigfoot. Stinks like a skunk. Not very intelligent. Can't speak but makes grunting noises. Might eat people. Found in forests and mountainous areas all over the world.

∞∞∞

Everyone was silent. They were all shocked, even Hugo.

"But we don't eat people," Pip said finally, in a hurt voice. "We don't eat meat at all."

"Unlike Humans," Roderick grumbled. "Humans will eat just about anything."

"And we don't make grunting noises," said Malcolm.

"Of course not!" said Boone quickly. "These are just dumb old cards."

"Do Humans really think we're monsters?" Pip asked Boone.

"I guess some Humans do—" Boone started to say.

"Well, that's just . . . that's just . . . awful!" Pip said angrily, and she shoved her stack of cards back at Boone and stomped off.

"I dek bads eber day," said Izzy before handing back his cards and walking away.

"What did he say?" asked Boone.

"He said, 'I take baths every day,' " Hugo translated.

The other squidges left, too. Even Gigi quietly slipped away.

"Wait, guys ... *I* don't think Sasquatches are monsters!" Boone called out to them, but everyone pretended not to hear him.

Hugo put his arm around Boone's shoulder.

"Don't worry, Boone. They'll get used to you. Remember, this is the first day a Human has ever gone to our school."

And I hope it's not the last day, too, Hugo couldn't help thinking.

9

Mrs. Nukluk's Big Surprise

After recess, Mrs. Nukluk said that it was time for the big surprise. She stepped out of the room to go get it. Pip made a squeak of excitement, while Izzy bounced in his chair. Even Hugo had forgotten to be upset about Boone and was now staring at the door, eagerly waiting for Mrs. Nukluk's surprise.

"I bet it's a trampoline," said Malcolm.

"Shhh!" Gigi said. "If she catches us talking she won't give us the surprise at all."

They heard Mrs. Nukluk's thumping footsteps coming back down the hall. Everyone sat up straight in their chairs.

After a minute Mrs. Nukluk walked into the classroom carrying a very large wooden crate. On the front of the crate, it said CAUTION! LIVE CARGO!

"It's the crate from the post office!" Hugo cried, before he could stop himself.

"*Shhhh*!" all the squidges told him.

Mrs. Nukluk placed the crate on the floor. She smoothed down the goose feathers on her cloak, then looked at all of them and smiled.

"Is everyone ready for the surprise?" she asked.

"*YEEESSSS*!" they all shouted.

Mrs. Nukluk squinched up her eyes and stuck her fingers in her ears. But she was still smiling, so it was okay.

"Well, I thought it was finally time for us to have . . . our . . . very . . . own . . ." She was speaking slowly to stretch out the suspense. Everyone squirmed in their chairs.

"Let it be a microscope, let it be a microscope," Hugo heard Gigi saying under her breath.

"Our very own class pet!" Mrs. Nukluk finished.

The whole class made a whoop of joy, even Boone. The Academy for Curious Squidges had never had a class pet before. Sometimes a mouse would wander into the classroom, then wander out again, but that was not the same thing.

"Is it a camel?" asked Malcolm. But a

camel in a cavern was too ridiculous, so no one even answered him.

Carefully, Mrs. Nukluk removed the top of the wooden crate. All the squidges leaned forward in their seats to try to see inside. Reaching into the crate, Mrs. Nukluk pulled out a large glass aquarium tank. She placed it on top of her desk. Inside the glass tank were wood chips, a wooden hut, some wooden bowls, and what looked like two hairy snowballs with long ears.

"*Ooooo!* What are they?" asked Pip.

"They are called Arctic Floofs," said Mrs. Nukluk.

"They look like guinea pigs, except with rabbit ears," said Boone.

Which was exactly what they looked like.

There were all kinds of questions after that, like:

What do we feed them? (Berries and leaves.)

Do they bite? (Only if you bite them first.)

Are the Floofs married? (That was Malcolm's question, and the answer was a deep breath from Mrs. Nukluk.)

Hugo had never had a pet before. He always thought it might be nice to have a pet bat. There were plenty of bats in Widdershins Cavern. He thought they were cute, with their little fox-faces, but he knew his mom would never let a bat live in his bedroom.

Hugo raised his hand.

"Can I hold one of the Floofs?" he asked.

And then, of course, the whole class wanted to hold them.

Mrs. Nukluk scooped one of the Floofs out of the tank. It made a funny little squeaking noise. Carefully, she put it in Hugo's hands. The Floof was warm, and its fur was silky soft. Hugo felt the Floof's heartbeat against the palm of his hand. With one finger he gently pet its little head, and the Floof made its squeaking sound again.

"He likes you," Gigi said.

Hugo sighed happily. An Arctic Floof was even better than a bat.

He sniffed its fur. "It smells like warm biscuits," he said.

After a moment, Mrs. Nukluk took the Floof from Hugo, much to Hugo's disappointment, and put it into Gigi's hands.

"We'll have to name them, of course," said Mrs. Nukluk.

"How about Cha Cha and Bumbles?" suggested Hugo.

"The names should rhyme," said Gigi. "How about Benny and Penny?"

"Or Mollie and Ollie?" said Pip.

"Or Lucus and Mucus," suggested Malcolm.

They argued over the names as the little Floof was passed around the class.

Finally, Mrs. Nukluk came to Boone. Boone cupped his hands together and held them out. Mrs. Nukluk put the Floof in them.

"Hello, little guy," he said to it softly. "Or girl."

Boone stared down at the Floof. It looked back up at him with its shiny black eyes.

Boone bent his head down and pressed his nose to the Floof's fur, sniffing in the warm biscuit smell.

"*Mrs. Nukluk!!*" shrieked Roderick. "*Stop him, Mrs. Nukluk! Boone is trying to eat the Floof!*"

"No, I'm not!" cried Boone.

"Yes, you were! You were just about to take a bite out of him!" insisted Roderick.

"I'm sure you're mistaken, Roderick," said Mrs. Nukluk.

"I'm sitting right next to him! I can see better than anybody. He opened his mouth like this." Roderick opened his mouth wide enough to fit a Floof in it.

The class gasped.

"I only wanted to sniff him," Boone said. He looked around the class at all the horrified faces. "Because he smells like biscuits . . ."

Okay, here's the part that I don't want to tell you. But I feel like I need to be perfectly honest. Hugo's face was horrified, too. Because even though Hugo didn't *really* think Boone would ever eat a Floof, he remembered what Roderick had said about Humans eating just about anything.

And though Hugo didn't *really* think that Boone had opened his mouth to take a bite out of the Floof, Boone *had* put his face awfully close to it . . .

Hugo looked at Boone. Boone looked back at Hugo, and he saw the shocked expression on his friend's face. Boone sighed. With the Floof still cupped in his hands, he stood up and walked to the front of the classroom. Very carefully, he handed the Floof back to Mrs. Nukluk.

"I think I'd better go home now," he said.

"Oh, Boone," said Mrs. Nukluk. "I'm sure we can work this out."

"Thanks anyway, Mrs. Nukluk." He put

out his hand. Mrs. Nukluk took it in her large hairy hand and shook it.

Then, after a sad little half-wave to Hugo, Boone headed out of the classroom. All the squidges turned around to watch him leave.

That's when two things happened:

1. Hugo's Monster Detector started to go *CLICK-CLICK-CLICK-CLICK!*

2. Everyone saw a grizzly green beast rush through the hallway outside the school.

10

The Adventures of Big Foot and Little Foot

I t's the Green Whistler!" cried Hugo.

The squidges screamed and jumped to their feet.

"Sit down, everyone!" ordered Mrs. Nukluk. "We'll all stay right here until that creature is caught."

"What will they do to it when they catch

it?" asked Boone, who was still standing near the door.

"I'm not sure, Boone," said Mrs. Nukluk. "Now come back in the classroom please."

But Boone shook his head. "Mrs. Nukluk, I am going to be a cryptozoologist," he said stoutly. "And that thing out there is a cryptid, so I have to help it if I can." Then he turned and dashed out the door.

It took Hugo a second to decide what he needed to do. Boone was his best friend. He had once saved Hugo from drowning in the Ripple Worm River. They were Big Foot and Little Foot, future cryptozoologists! If Boone was going after the Green Whistler, Hugo was, too.

He leapt out of his seat and ran out of the classroom. Behind him, he could hear Mrs. Nukluk yelling for him to come back. He knew he was going to be in big trouble. He kept going anyway.

"Wait for me, Boone!" he called when he spied Boone up ahead in a passageway. "I'm coming with you!"

Boone turned around, surprised to see Hugo.

"Are you sure?" Boone asked.

"I'm totally sure," Hugo replied.

Once again, I have to be honest with you. Hugo was not *totally* sure. He was only *mostly* sure. After all, they were chasing a dangerous monster. And on top of that, the monster might be a

squidge-eating monster, so you can't really blame Hugo for being a tiny bit not sure.

Hugo and Boone hurried along the passageway as quietly as possible. A few times, Boone's sneakers slapped against the floor, but Hugo's bare feet did not make a sound. Neither did the Monster Detector. That meant the Green Whistler was not nearby. Secretly, Hugo felt relieved.

The passageway widened, then narrowed, then twisted and turned. Hugo kept listening for the *click-click* of the Monster Detector or, even worse, the dreaded whistle of the Green Whistler. But the only sound he heard was the growling of his own stomach. It made him think of the acorn butter–and–raspberry cream sandwiches still sitting in his lunch bag back at school.

"Maybe the Green Whistler went a different way," Hugo said hopefully.

"Maybe," Boone said.

"Or it might have left the cavern altogether," Hugo said, his voice brightening.

But then they heard it:

Click-click-click.

Hugo looked down at his wrist. The weechie-weechie moths were flapping their wings. Hugo felt a lump of dread in the place where his acorn butter–and–raspberry cream sandwiches should have been.

"Does that mean what I think it means?" Boone asked.

Hugo nodded.

Boone smiled.

With a deep but whispery voice, Boone said, "In the dark, spooky cavern, Big Foot and Little Foot were hot on the trail of the legendary Green Whistler."

"What?" Hugo was confused.

In his regular voice, Boone said, "This

will be a chapter in the book I'm going to write about us one day. You know . . . *The Adventures of Big Foot and Little Foot.*" He

glanced shyly at Hugo. "I mean . . . if you still think that we make a good team and all."

Hugo cleared his throat. In his deepest voice, he whispered, "Big Foot and Little Foot were so close to the monster they could smell it."

They really could smell it, too. There was a strange odor in the passageway—both sharp and musty. It made their noses wrinkle up.

Boone continued the story: "The cavern was swarming with poisonous snakes, hissing and slithering across their path." He looked over at Hugo, because this was sort of a lie.

"Nice touch," Hugo whispered approvingly.

Boone continued in his deep voice: "Still, they had to stop the beast before it hurt someone, or someone hurt it."

That was true, thought Hugo. Then he wondered out loud, "But how will we stop it?"

"I'm not sure yet," Boone said in his

regular Boone voice. "When the time comes, we'll know what to do." He said this with such confidence that Hugo felt certain Boone was right.

Hugo continued the story: "Even though there was danger all around them, Big Foot wasn't afraid, because Little Foot was with him. And Little Foot was the smartest, bravest, and best friend any squidge could ever have."

"Thanks, Hugo," Boone said quietly.

And that's when they knew everything would be okay between them.

11

Twists and Turns

Every so often the passageway split into two, and they had to figure out which way to go. They would try one passage, and if the Monster Detector stopped clicking, they would turn back and go the other way.

After a while, Boone asked, "Do you know where we are?"

Hugo looked all around him. Nothing was familiar.

"I'm not sure," Hugo answered.

The cavern was very large, and they had traveled through so many twists and turns that Hugo had lost track. Now Hugo remembered all the times he and Winnie were warned not to go wandering in the cavern. If they got lost, their mom and dad told them, it might be hours, or even days, before they were found again.

Or maybe never, a little voice in his head said. They'd be lost and alone with a squidge-eating monster on the loose!

Suddenly, Hugo stopped walking. He sniffed the air.

"Do you smell something?" Hugo asked.

"I can still smell the Green Whistler," Boone said.

"No," said Hugo, "something else."

Boone sniffed the air, then shook his head.

"I don't smell it," he said.

But Sasquatches are very good sniffers, much better than Humans. Hugo *did* smell something. It smelled like onions and the North Woods on a cool autumn day.

Up ahead, the passageway took a sharp turn to the right. As they approached the turn, the Monster Detector started *click-click-clicking* faster and faster. Just as Hugo and Boone rounded the bend, they saw something move in the distance.

There it was. The Green Whistler.

In the darkness, they could see the hulking shadowy figure lumbering along. Suddenly, the beast stopped and spun around. It was too dim to make out its face, but they could see the shine of its eyes.

"It sees us," Boone whispered.

Hugo nodded, but was too scared to whisper back.

The Green Whistler turned, and in a flash it disappeared through an open doorway just ahead of it.

Hugo sniffed the air again. The oniony, woodsy smell was even stronger.

Now Hugo knew what that smell was. It was a mushroom tart, just out of the oven. *And* he knew exactly where they were!

"Hurry, hurry!" Hugo cried. He took off running at top speed, with Boone close behind him. They ran down the passageway and through the open doorway . . . which just so happened to be the back door to the kitchen at the Everything-You-Need General Store and Bakery.

12

The Dreaded Whistle

The Green Whistler was standing with its back to them, looking at Hugo's grandpa. The monster's green fur was mangy and ratty. Hugo could hear its wheezing breath and could smell its sharp, stinging stench.

Grandpa was holding a steaming mushroom tart, staring back at the monster in shock.

"How? I don't . . . it's impossible . . ." Grandpa sputtered.

That's when the absolute worst thing happened.

The Green Whistler began to whistle.

The whistle was high-pitched, and it swooped up and down, almost like a song. Grandpa opened his mouth as though he was going to say something, but no words came out. Hugo's heart was thumping hard as he watched the Green Whistler move toward Grandpa. Any minute now, it was going to pounce.

"Do we know what to do yet?" Hugo said to Boone in a panicky voice.

"Yup," said Boone easily.

Boone walked right up to the monster.

Before Hugo could stop him, Boone threw his arms around it and hugged it. He hugged it so hard that the Green Whistler said, "Ow, Boone, you're squeezing! And for heaven's sake, what are you doing here?"

"What are *you* doing here, Grandma?" asked Boone.

Because that was who the Green Whistler was. Only you wouldn't have known it, because she was wrapped in the wooliest green blanket you'd ever seen.

"She's here to see me," said Grandpa, smiling fondly at Boone's grandma. "Now get some plates out of the cupboard, Hugo. Nothing goes better with a long explanation than a slice of mushroom tart."

13

Explanations

After Boone explained to his grandma about squidge school, he folded his arms and said to her, "Okay, your turn."

Boone's grandma swallowed her bite of mushroom tart and began: "When I was right about your age, Boone, and just as sassy—"

"And when I was a young squidge, a little older than Hugo," added Grandpa, "Ruthie and I ran into each other in the North Woods by accident."

"Do you know what he said to me when he first saw me?" Grandma Ruthie jerked a thumb toward Grandpa. "He said that I looked like a plucked turkey in a dress."

"Well, I'd never seen a Human before," said Grandpa.

"Anyway, I forgave him. Wasn't that big of me? And besides, I thought he looked like an overgrown gorilla. In the end, we became best friends."

"Like Boone and me," said Hugo.

"Exactly," said Grandpa. "We used to meet in secret, in a little room in the west

part of the cavern. I'd know she was there

because she would whistle for me."

Grandma Ruthie whistled the same tune she had whistled a few minutes before.

"I recognized that whistle," Boone told Hugo. "That's when I knew the Green Whistler was Grandma. She always whistles like that for me when I'm outside and she wants me to come in for dinner."

"Yes, and you always pretend you don't hear," she said to Boone, reaching out and giving his ear a tweak.

"Ruthie would bring a picnic lunch and a blanket," continued Grandpa, "and

we would sit in our secret room and talk and laugh and play games for hours. She taught me how to play poker."

"I always won," Grandma Ruthie said.

Grandpa leaned over to Hugo and Boone and said quietly, "I think she cheated."

"Oh, I did!" Grandma Ruthie said, laughing.

"We had the best time, didn't we?" Grandpa said to her.

"The best," she agreed. Then her face grew serious. "Until one day . . ."

"Oh yes," Grandpa's face grew serious, too.

"One day, I was waiting in the room with my picnic lunch and my blanket, whistling for your Grandpa. I was hungry, so between whistles, I nibbled on some fried chicken—"

"Disgusting stuff!" Grandpa said.

"Well, I always brought jelly sandwiches for you, didn't I? Anyway, right then a Sasquatch was walking outside, and he heard me whistling. I spotted him just in time. Right before he peeped into the

room, I threw the blanket over my head—yes, it was that very same green blanket. Well, that Sasquatch took one look at me under the green blanket, and then he saw the chicken bones on the ground, and he took off running."

"That's how the story of the Green Whistler got started," said Grandpa.

"Soon after that, my family moved to the city. We packed up and left, and I never even had a chance to say good-bye to my friend."

"Ah, so that's what happened," Grandpa said. "I had always wondered."

"Is that why we moved to the North Woods, Grandma?" Boone asked. "So you could find Hugo's grandfather?"

"Don't be silly," Grandma Ruthie said. "We moved here for the peace and quiet, and because a childhood in the woods is the best sort of childhood of all." Then she smiled at Hugo's grandfather. "*And* we moved here so that I could find my dear old friend again . . . and beat him in a few rounds of poker."

14

The Green Blanket

It was then that Hugo realized something.

"I guess my Monster Detector never really worked after all, since you're not a monster," he said to Grandma Ruthie.

"I should say not," she replied.

Hugo undid the strap and tossed the Monster Detector on the table in disgust.

"I collected all those Monster Card wrappers for nothing."

Grandma Ruthie picked up the Monster Detector and examined it with great interest.

"What are those little white specks behind the glass?" she asked.

"They're called weechie-weechie moths," said Hugo. "They were clicking like crazy the whole time we were following you."

"*Ahhh*!" Grandma Ruthie said as though she understood something now. Taking the Monster Detector, she went over to her green blanket, which she had left on a stool in the corner.

Click-click, went the Monster Detector.

CLICK-CLICK-CLICK!!! CLICK-CLICK-CLICK!!!

"See!" said Hugo. "It doesn't work. The blanket isn't a monster."

"Maybe not to you, but it is to the weechie-weechie moths," Grandma Ruthie said. "Haven't you noticed the smell?" She picked up the mangy-looking blanket and brought it over to them.

Hugo, Boone, and Grandpa all wrinkled their noses at the sharp, musty stench.

"We thought that was the smell of the Green Whistler," said Boone.

"It's the smell of mothballs!" said Grandma Ruthie. "I stored the blanket with them. Moths hate the smell of mothballs!"

The weechie-weechie moths were flapping their wings so frantically that Hugo took the Monster Detector from Grandma Ruthie, just to rescue them. He put the Monster Detector back on his wrist. He'd grown sort of fond of the weechie-weechie moths. They might even make pretty good pets, he thought.

"Ruthie, why on earth were you running around with that nasty blanket over you anyway?" asked Grandpa.

"I always wear it when I come to the cavern," she said.

"You mean you've been here before?"

"Many times. I waited in our secret room, but you never showed up. So I figured I'd snoop around the cavern. I knew the other Sasquatches would run away from me if I was dressed like the Green Whistler. Sasquatches are such scaredy-cats!"

"Not Hugo," Boone said. "He's brave."

"Well, maybe not *totally* brave," Hugo confessed. "I think I'm just *mostly* brave."

"So . . ." Grandma Ruthie turned to Grandpa. "Do you think a plucked turkey and an overgrown gorilla can still be friends?"

"I'm certain of it," Grandpa said.

15

Floating Post Office

hen Hugo got back home that day he went straight to his room.

There was a little stream that ran right into Hugo's bedroom through a hole in the bottom of the wall. It wiggled across the room and then went out another hole in the wall by Hugo's toy chest. In a funny way, that little stream was Hugo and Boone's personal floating post office, since that's how they sent messages to each other.

Opening up his toy chest, Hugo pulled out a little wooden boat. He had carved it himself, and it could float as well as a boat twenty times its size. This is the note that Hugo wrote to Boone:

HI, BOONE.

WHEN I WENT BACK TO CLASS TODAY, MRS. NUKLUK WAS PRETTY MAD AT ME FOR LEAVING. BUT WHEN I TOLD HER ABOUT WHAT HAPPENED, SHE SAID IF I WROTE IT ALL OUT IN MY BEST HANDWRITING, IT WOULD COUNT FOR THE ENGLISH CLASS THAT I MISSED. I EVEN INCLUDED THE PART ABOUT THE POISONOUS SNAKES. HA-HA!

ALSO, GUESS WHAT? THE SQUIDGES WANT YOU TO COME BACK TO OUR SCHOOL! THEY SAID ANYONE WHO WOULD RUN OFF TO HELP A MONSTER WOULD NEVER EAT A FLOOF (WELL, RODERICK WASN'T CONVINCED, BUT TOO BAD FOR HIM). SO PLEASE COME BACK TO SCHOOL, BOONE. THINK OF ALL THE ADVENTURES WE COULD HAVE IF WE SAW EACH OTHER EVERY DAY!

YOUR FRIEND ALWAYS,

HUGO

Hugo rolled up the note and put it in a little glass bottle with a stopper. He put the bottle in the toy boat and carefully placed the boat on the stream. Then he took a deep breath and blew it out on the little boat's stern. The boat wobbled at first before it floated down the stream, through the little hole in the wall, and out into the Big Wide World.

16

Blueberry Ink

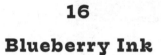

The next day, however, Boone was not at school.

Hugo was crestfallen. Even though Boone had only been at the Academy for Curious Squidges for one day, the classroom just wasn't the same without him. The empty seat beside Roderick seemed like it was waiting for

Boone to sit in it. Even helping to name the Floofs didn't cheer Hugo up. (The class finally settled on the names Daisy and Mr. Biggles.)

Art class was first. They were learning how to make ink out of blueberries. It was something Hugo had been looking forward to doing for weeks, but he just couldn't feel happy about anything today.

Mrs. Nukluk gave everyone a wooden bowl full of blueberries and a wooden pestle. The first thing they had to do was smash all the berries to get the juice out of them. The squidges smashed and bashed so loudly that no one heard the footsteps running down the hall outside the school and into the classroom.

"Sorry I'm late!" a voice cried from the back of the room.

Everyone turned around and there was Boone, with his thirty-eight freckles and his brown paper bag.

"You're here!" cried Hugo.

"Of course. I would have come sooner, but I just got your note a few minutes ago," said Boone. "The river's current is running a little slow."

Which, by the way, is one of the drawbacks of a floating post office.

"Mrs. Nukluk," said Boone, "if it's okay with you, I'd like to go to squidge school. I don't know a lot about snuds and stuff like that, but I'm a quick learner."

"Boone, we would be *honored* to have you in our class," said Mrs. Nukluk.

The whole class cheered. Well, everyone except Roderick, but he didn't yell "Boo!" or anything like that either. Some squidges (and people, too) just take a little longer to change their minds about things.

Right then Hugo had an idea. He raised his hand, then waved it around to show that he had something extra important to say.

"Yes, Hugo?"

"I have an idea," Hugo said.

"What is it?" Mrs. Nukluk asked.

"I don't want to say it out loud."

Mrs. Nukluk considered. "You can come up here and whisper it to me."

Hugo walked up to Mrs. Nukluk's desk. He leaned close to her ear. He had never

been that close to Mrs. Nukluk's head before. It smelled like bananas.

Hugo cupped his hand around his
mouth and whispered his idea into Mrs.
Nukluk's ear. Then he leaned away so he
could see her face. It looked happy.

"That's an *excellent* idea, Hugo," she
said.

"Thanks," Hugo said. "Can I whisper something else?"

"All right."

Hugo cupped his hand and leaned close. He didn't really have anything else to say. He just wanted to smell her head again. But since he had to say *something*, he asked, "Why does your head smell like bananas?"

Mrs. Nukluk looked at him. He looked back at her. Then she leaned over and whispered in his ear, "Banana shampoo."

Hugo nodded. "Got it," he said.

Mrs. Nukluk liked Hugo's idea so much that she went right to the art closet and gathered up all the supplies. Then, without telling the class why, she led everyone out of the classroom and into the hallway just outside the school's entrance.

Hugo climbed onto Mrs. Nukluk's shoulders. Mrs. Nukluk climbed on a chair. She handed Hugo a container of blueberry ink and a pine-needle paintbrush. In his best, most careful handwriting, Hugo added two new words to the school sign:

ACKNOWLEDGMENTS

Sasquatches know that we all need help if we want to do things right, and that's why I want to thank my wonderful "Sasquatch Community." Major thanks to my editor, Erica Finkel, for her clear-sighted wisdom. I am forever grateful to my agent, Alice Tasman, who is even better than thirty jars of acorn butter. Thanks to Felicita Sala for bringing Hugo and his friends to life with her beautiful illustrations. Big thanks to my publicist, Kimberley Moran, and the entire Abrams team for spreading the word about Hugo and Boone. And finally, as always, thanks to my practically perfect husband, Adam, and my own squidge, Ian.

The adventures of

BIG FÖÖT
and LITTLE FÖÖT

continue in book three:

THE SQUATCHICORNS

Turn the page for a sneak peek!

1

Castles & Knights

Deep in the cold North Woods there lived a young Sasquatch named Hugo. He was bigger than you but smaller than me, and he was hairier than both of us. He lived in apartment 1G in the very back of Widdershins Cavern with his mother and father and his older sister, Winnie.

It was Saturday morning, and Hugo and his friend Gigi were sitting on the floor playing a game they had made up called Castles & Knights. They used cups turned upside down for the castles. For the roads, they used sticks, and they had painted faces on rocks for their characters. There

were smooth bits of red and green and blue glass that Hugo's grandpa had found in the woods while hunting mushrooms—these were the magic gems.

"My knight is crossing the moat to attack your castle," Gigi said, pushing a painted rock forward.

"Okay, then my wizard is going to open the secret trapdoor," Hugo said, "and a Snallygaster is going to fly out and attack your knight."

Gigi looked at Hugo.

"A Snallygaster? You can't make up creatures out of your head, Hugo. Maybe you could use a dragon. Or a Minotaur."

"But there really is such a thing as a Snallygaster! Hold on, I'll prove it."

Hugo got up and walked over to his bookshelf.

Rick-a-tick-a-tick.

Gigi frowned at the sound.

From the bookshelf, Hugo pulled out a very thick hardcover book called *The Biggest Ever Book of Cryptids*. His best friend, Boone, had lent the book to him, and Hugo had been reading it every day. Even when it was past his bedtime, he would read the book under his blankets, using his jar of glowworms for light. The book listed all the known cryptids (which is a fancy word for "mysterious creatures") in alphabetical order. It had full-color illustrations of each one of them, too. Once in a while, there was a photograph of a cryptid, but those

were usually pretty blurry and could just as easily have been something else.

Hugo walked back to Gigi to show her the book.

Rick-a-tick-a-tick.

"Hugo," Gigi said, staring down at Hugo's feet, "when was the last time you cut your toenails?"

"I don't know. Why?" Hugo sat down beside her and leafed through the book to find the section about Snallygasters.

"Because your toenails are so long that they're clicking against the ground."

Hugo ignored this. He flipped through

the pages, past pictures of creatures that he had never heard of before reading the book. There was an Owlman and Swamp Monsters and Tommyknockers and Globsters. Some of the creatures were no bigger than a pinkie toe, and others were taller than the tallest pine tree.

"Snallygaster! Here it is!" Hugo pointed at a page with a picture of a snaky-looking beast. He read, "'A dragon-like creature that is half bird, half reptile, with razor-sharp teeth.' There! I told you they were a real thing!"

Right then they heard the noise again. *Rick-a-tick-a-tick.*

"Well, that's obviously not my toe-nails," Hugo told Gigi.

Hugo stood up and walked over to the little stream that ran right through his bedroom. It entered the room through a hole in the bottom of the wall, then it wiggled across the room and exited through another hole in the wall by Hugo's toy chest. The little stream was

Hugo's personal floating post office, since that's how he and Boone sent messages to each other.

Rick-a-tick-a-tick.

A wooden toy boat sailed through the hole in the wall and into Hugo's room. A little bottle was *rick-a-tick-a-ticking* around inside the boat. And in that bottle was a note from Boone.

ELLEN POTTER is the award-winning author of many books for children, including the Olivia Kidney series, *Slob*, *The Kneebone Boy*, and most recently, the Piper Green and the Fairy Tree series. She lives in Maine.

FELICITA SALA is a self-taught illustrator of many books for children. She lives with her husband and daughter in Rome, Italy.

READ THESE OTHER GREAT CHAPTER BOOKS!

TABLE OF CONTENTS

WHAT IS THE MEDITATIONS WITH SERIES?

Bear & Co. is publishing this series of creation-centered mystic/prophets to bring to the attention and prayer of peoples today the power and energy of the holistic mystics of the western tradition. One reason western culture succumbs to boredom and to violence is that we are not being challenged by our religious traditions to be all we can be. This is also the reason that many sincere spiritual seekers go East for their mysticism — because the West is itself out of touch with its deepest spiritual guides. The format Bear & Co. has chosen in which to present these holistic mystic/prophets is deliberate: We do not feel that more academically-styled books on our mystics is what every-day believers need: Rather, we wish to get the mystics of personal and social transformation off our dusty shelves and into the hearts and minds and bodies of our people. To do this we choose a format that is ideal for meditation, for imaging, for sharing in groups and in prayer occasions. We rely on primary sources for the texts but we let the author's words and images flow from her or his inner structure to our deep inner selves.

OTHER BOOKS IN THE
MEDITATIONS WITH
SERIES

Mechtild of Magdeburg
JULIAN of NORWICH
MEISTER ECKHART

Coming soon

THERESA of AVILA
JOHN of the CROSS

PREFACE

Two years ago, on the 1500th anniversary of St. Benedict, I was invited to celebrate the occasion with a team of about 135 Benedictine men and women. They invited me to come to speak for a day on spirituality and I chose as my topic the spirituality of Hildegard of Bingen, one of the greatest thinkers and doers of the Western church. I felt that Hildegard's brothers and sisters could easily ignore what I had to say but would be hard put to ignore one of their own. I took an informal poll and found, to my surprise, that only about 15% of those present had heard of Hildegard at all. When I completed the day a very old nun who was blind and stoop-backed and dressed in complete black habit and who was beautiful came up to me and said: "Isn't it a scandal that a Dominican had to come and teach us about Hildegard? I heard of her in novitiate 62 years ago—and no one has mentioned her since." When I pressed some of the women Benedictines further on why they did not know Hildegard I was told that "we only studied the male saints of our Order."

This is indeed a scandal—namely that Westerners and even Benedictines know Augustine and no doubt Thomas a Kempis and Tanquerry and other Fall/Redemption theologians inside out—but do not know Hildegard. Hildegard can be called the Grandmother of the Rhineland mystic movement, a movement of creation-centered spirituality. The year of her death (1179) St. Francis of Assisi was born; there followed Thomas Aquinas, Mechtild of Magdeburg, Meister Eckhart, the anonymous author of the *Theologica Germanica* and Julian of Norwich. It is doubtful that any of these mystic-prophets would have sunk so deeply into truth and experience had St. Hildegard not preceded them. This great renaissance woman—musician and poet, dramatist and physicist, doctor and prophet, painter and leader of both women and men, lover of the earth and all creation, can no longer be ignored. She represents the big link between Christian Spirituality and pre-patriarchal spiritualities. This book represents the very first time that Hildegard's words have appeared in the English language.

7

That she has been so utterly ignored in church circles is typical of the fate of other creation-centered mystics such as Julian of Norwich, Mechtild of Magdeburg and Meister Eckhart. When one reads and prays the wisdom and the passion, the insight and the humor, that Hildegard shares in these pages one will realize once again what a horrible thing religion has done in the West in exiling creation theology in favor of an almost exclusively Fall/Redemption spirituality. It is interesting to me that while religious publishing houses continue to turn out more and more editions of the dualistic spiritualities of the West (for example, still more editions of Bonaventure's *Life of St. Francis* or Thomas á Kempis' *Imitation of Christ*) the more 'profane' world as represented, for example, by artist Judy Chicago or the chorus of the University of Arkansas* are not ignoring Hildegard of Bingen.

Why is this that searchers into women's stories and into the story of western music are drawn to Hildegard today? I have no doubt that it is because her spirituality speaks to a dangerous vacuum in the hearts and minds of spiritual journeyers in the West. Here, briefly, I would like to recount a few of Hildegard's accomplishments in spirituality that speak so deeply to today's needs.

1) A psychology of Microcosm/Macrocosm. When C.G. Jung comments that the proper psychology for twentieth century persons is medieval psychology, I believe he has in mind the fact that ego psychologies are not adequate to the spiritual demands on our psyches. What is needed is a micro/macrocosmic view of ourselves, of the universe. What is essential is relationships—all of them. And this is truly the basic pattern of self-understanding in Hildegard's world view. Hildegard says: "The air, blowing everywhere, serves all creatures." This sense of cosmic interdependence wafts throughout all her work. For Hildegard a theology of the Word is not about words, footnotes and books. It is about all creatures, all creativity. "The WORD is living, being, spirit, all verdant greening, all creativity. This WORD manifests itself in every creature" she sings. Creation is a profound and divine blessing, divinely blessed—"the entire world has been embraced by the Creator's kiss" she declares. Hildegard believes that the wonderful harmony and balance of things in creation is "sufficient"—here lies the end of greed and rapacious life styles. It comes with knowing when enough is enough. And Hildegard believed that nature teaches such wisdom. Further, Hildegard

believed in the interdependence of all micro/macrocosm, for "God has arranged all things in the world in consideration of everything else." A grounding in peaceful and gentle ways of living emerges from such faith as Hildegard writes about. Hildegard's is not a religious psychology of fear or of guilt but of trust. "Trust shows the way" she declares. And this trust is a trust of creation around one as well as within one, a trust of cosmos as well as that cosmos-within-a-cosmos which is oneself.

2) A grounding in earth and earthiness. Hildegard practices what she preaches—she trusts the earth including her own earthiness and sensuousness. "The earth is mother of all that is natural, mother of all that is human." Humankind itself is an "earth" that "contains all moistness, all verdancy, all germinating power." From the earth came the "substance of the incarnation of God's son." Hildegard, in distinction from Augustine who wrote that "the soul makes war with the body", was at home with her earthiness and sexuality. She proclaims loudly the beauty of sexuality and marriage—indeed if her theology had been followed in both Protestant and Catholic churches in the West we would have a much sounder practice of sensual spirituality and of marriage as sacrament than we do today. And a true reverence for the human body. Hildegard sings: "Holy persons draw to themselves all that is earthly." Clearly there is no spirit/matter dualism in this wonderful woman. In fact, her images for the fullest human and spiritual living are inevitably images of being fruitful as all earth creatures are meant to be. "Become a flowering orchard" she exclaims. How does one do this? "This person who does good works is indeed this orchard bearing good fruit. And this is just like the earth with its ornamentation of stones and blossoming trees."

Hildegard talks often of the "sweating power" of the earth, of the need to stay juicy, wet, green, moist and also good humored. It is good—and alas, all to rare—to hear a theologian of the West talk of "the juice of creation," the "juice" of the soul and of humanity's works. Hildegard's is a juicy—not a dry—theology.

3) A non-trivial understanding of sin. Because Hildegard and the rest of the creation-centered spiritual tradition is not haunted by a bad conscience and is not overly introspective and thus overly anthropomorphic in her relating to God and creation, and because she is not dualistic as regards body and soul, passion and grace, earth and spirit, Hildegard's theology of sin is not a trivial

9

matter. Hildegard, like other creation-centered theologians, does not begin her theology with sin—not even with original sin. But this does not mean she lacks insight and depth as to the meaning and the cure of human sinning. If creation is a cosmic blessing, then true sin represents a rupture in the cosmos, a rupture in relationships. "Creation blooms and flourishes when it remains in right relationship and keeps to its assigned tasks" she declares. The breaking of right relationship is injustice and all injustice represents a rupture in the cosmos itself. "Without nature, humankind cannot survive" she warns us—a particularly timely warning for our times of nuclear threat. The following lament sounds like Hildegard might have been present in Hiroshima or Nagasaki. Or at Three Mile Island. Or at Love Canal.

> Now in the people that were meant to be green, there is no more life of any kind. There is only shrivelled barrenness. The winds are burdened by the utterly awful stink of evil, selfish goings-on. Thunderstorms menace.

> The air belches out the filthy uncleanliness of the peoples. There pours forth an unnatural, a loathsome darkness, that withers the green, and wizens the fruit that was to serve as food for the people.

> Sometimes this layer of air is full, full of a fog that is the source of many destructive and barren creatures that destroy and damage the earth, rendering it incapable of sustaining humanity.

The ultimate sin, Hildegard recognizes, is ecological: A sin against the earth, against the air, against the waters, against God's creation—for in injuring creation's interdependent balance we are destroying all life including our own. Hildegard shouts to us through eight centuries of silence: "The earth should not be injured. The earth should not be destroyed." And she warns humankind of the result—not that individuals ought to be afraid of a private hell but because creation itself seeks a balance and keeps a record of how it is treated that no human power can cover up. "If the elements of the world are violated by ill-treatment," she warns, "God will cleanse them through the sufferings and the hardships of humankind." If we misuse the "privilege" that creation is, then "God's justice permits creation to punish humanity."

We see here how Hildegard's is a theology of liberation wherein

10

creation itself is being liberated and with it, by learning wisdom and just living, humanity is liberated. It is a liberation of all or of none. A cosmic liberation such as Paul wrote about in Romans 8 and Chief Seattle preached about in America's northwest.

In this modest preface I have alluded briefly to only three of the rich contributions Hildegard makes to our spiritual lives today. The reader will find much, much more both in this book and in those others of this series of Meditations With Creation Centered Mystics. Let us not forget that in many respects Hildegard was the first of this vital — and far too often ignored — tradition in the West. I celebrate her return in our midst in this format that encourages prayer and sharing and that has proved so useful and non-elitest in the other volumes of this series. I thank Gabriele Uhlein for making Hildegard so available to us today and Thomas Berry who is clearly so near a brother to Sister Hildegard of Bingen.

Matthew Fox, op
Institute in Creation-Centered
Spirituality
Mundelein College, Chicago, Il.
Holy Names College, Oakland, CA.

Footnote

*Judy Chicago, The Dinner Party. An art exhibit on the history of women in the West. Hildegard von Bingen: Kyrie Eleison. Arkansas Univ. (Fayetteville) Schola Cantorum. Leonarda Productions, P.O. Box 124, Radio City Station, New York, NY 10101.

11

FORWARD

Hildegard of Bingen had a special intimacy with the natural world. She was not attracted to the divine in its pure transcendence as are many of the mystics. Nor was she preoccupied with the human world directly in its psychological problems of integration or with the problems of social reconciliation.

She avoided the basic difficulties that emerge from the recent emphasis on the two aspects of the mind, the intuitive-emotional and the rational-analytic. Neither of these allows for a third mode, the experiencing of life, of natural forms, the world of nature. The intuitive goes above the living world, the rational goes below it. This is a consequence of our western civilizational form. We function well in the world of the machine and in the world of the mind—even in the mind's deepest spiritual intuitions. At the same time we are incredibly alienated from any significant experience of those mysterious forces that are manifest in the sky and the sea and the land and in that fantastic variety of living beings that swim through the waters of earth and move over the land and fly through the air. We have no consciousness of forming a single community with all these members of planet earth. We are so alienated that we are well on our way to devastating the planet in a manner beyond all remedy from either heaven or earth. Extinction of genetic diversity of the earth is so absolute, so irreversible, that God himself could remedy the situation only by creating another planet or perhaps another universe.

We are rightly concerned with the nuclear bomb and with the blast, thermal, radiation and fall-out consequences it could produce. We should, however, be aware that we already are living amid the ruins of a still beautiful but severely damaged planet. Nor have we really seen the tragic consequences of our past deeds, consequences that cannot now be avoided. One naturalist is presently engaged in writing a book about the next few decades to be entitled *The Age of Slaughter* since the death-dealing deeds have already been accomplished. There remains only the interval before the full consequences are experienced.

13

To perceive the importance of Hildegard of Bingen we need to be aware of this present situation. The importance of any writer is largely determined by the historical period of the reader. We read differently from the reader in the baroque or the romantic or the realist periods of the past. We read in the period of environmental deterioration, of industrial decline, of social violence and of widespread personal alienation. But also we live in a new ecological age, an age when we are awakening to a new sense of the comprehensive community of all the living and non-living members of this glorious planet. This emerging period might be considered the Age of Renewal of Earth as a Bio-Spiritual Planet.

Thus far Christians have been so concerned with redemption out of this world, so attached to their spiritual life development or to their social mission of reconciliation that they have had little time for serious attention to the earth; nor do Christians seem to be aware of the futility of social transformations proceeding on an historical-industrial rather than on a comprehensive ecological basis. Whatever the reasons for this situation we find relatively few Christian guides in the past to enlighten or to inspire us to a more functional relationship between the human and the natural worlds.

Generally the two mentioned as models are Benedict with his agrarian model and Francis of Assisi with his model of the universal community of creatures. Hildegard might be considered as a third model with her sense of the earth as a region of delight. We might almost say of "pagan" delight since she has overcome the undesirable aspects of pagan naturalism not from without but from within the experience. She has reached far into the emotionally exciting aspects of nature in a unique mode of Christian communion. She sees the creation-maker in the ancient manner of the fertility cults, a view she expresses in her statement that creation and creator are related as a woman and man. Only thus is the earth fruitful. "I compare the great love of Creator and creation to the same love and fidelity with which God binds woman and man together. This is so that together they might be creatively fruitful." "The entire world has been embraced by this kiss." Because of this "erotic" bond the earth becomes luxuriant in its every aspect.

Thomas Berry
November 7, 1982

14

INTRODUCTION

In an age when it is easy to feel the wrath of God, Hildegard of Bingen would have us dare to feel God's pleasure. Living and dying almost 900 years ago in lush and beautiful Bavaria, she was poetess, abbess, musician, artist, healer, scientist, theologian, prophet and mystic par excellence. She attempted a most remarkable feat. Using a scholastic Latin that was cumbersome and rife with dualism, she presented a wholistic cosmology. Over and over again, Hildegard dared to speak of wholeness, of the complex interweavings of the human, the cosmic, and the divine in a many-splendored and deep oneness. Her secretary, Wilbert of Gembloux, himself appreciated the linguistic difficulty. Even then he remarked that his hope was that her readers not be like the donkey of German folk-lore, the donkey that merely carried the wine, without being able to taste a drop thereof.

...her spiritual grounding.

Even a cursory reading of Hildegard's writing reveals a spiritual tradition that is an alternative to the Fall-Redemption paradigm that has been our theological blinders for the last 1600 years. Hildegard is oriented toward a glorious celebration of life and affirms that living should be more than just recompense for original sin. The goodness of creation is at the very center of her theology, and the world is totally embraced by it. Further, in the mature development of this thought there is the largesse to embrace the dialectic, the both/and. Dualism is redeemed.

While oneness is indeed a mystic theme of Hildegard's, she does not superficially dismiss differences and polarities. She dares to depict the human being in truth, as creator and created; as gracious, compassionate and loving; but also as destroyer and destroyed; as malicious, obstinate, and self-indulgent. Further, the good and the bad, the light and the dark are recognized as ever present in a multitude of forms, hues and aromas for our senses to perceive. Hildegard makes it quite clear that to be human is to choose, to respond with awareness, to discern, and to act accordingly.

...her creative center.

Just how did this remarkable woman apprehend her own experience? The 77 year-old Hildegard wrote to a monk in response to this very question: "When and how I have the awareness I cannot say, but for as long as I have it, all sadness is taken from me, so that I feel like a young girl again, and not like an old woman." She goes on to describe herself as living in the shadow of the "Living Light." She writes that every now and then, within this shadowy cloud she would see the Living Light itself. In those instances she would receive the images and insights she was so to record for us. The visions were seen, as Hildegard described, in her spirit, not with external eyes, nor with any thoughts of her heart, nor with the help from her senses. Yet her outward eyes remained open and her bodily senses retained their activity.

These strong, vital spiritual encounters that nurtured her growth were further enhanced by the rapt attention she gave to the scriptures—specifically the Hebrew Scriptures. She was so steeped in Bible verses that she would quote them often and spontaneously to clarify the images in her own writings.

In regard to her own writings, Hildegard was well aware of her prophetic role: firstly, that she herself was dealing with the Word of God, and secondly, that it pleased the Creator to reveal it "not through a learned man, but rather wonderfully, through a simple and uneducated woman." Hildegard would also provide us with the criteriorn with which to approach the text. She understands that the fullness of her work can only be appreciated if one sets aside historical and philosophical categories and allows one's self to be "showered with the gentle raindrops of divine inspiration." In contemporary terms hers is a fine illustration of an intuitive "right-brain" method. Hildegard knows that God is delicious. Her fondest wish is for us to taste and see that goodness.

...her text.

A critical text of Hildegard's first book, *Scivias*, exists in Latin translation from Brepols, Turnhout, Antwerp Belgium (1978). This book contains thirty-six of her visions with commentaries on them and it forms the groundwork for her subsequent volumes. Among her other works are a book on nature, *Liber Physicae Elementorum*, a book on health, *Liber Compositae Medicinae*, a theological work on St. Athanasius, a commentary on the Gospels and an exposition on St. Benedict's rule. Now available in critical German editions from Otto Ruller Verlag in Salzburg are her other books: *Liber Vitae Meritorum* which deals with the co-creative accountability of humankind; *De Operatione Dei* which focuses on the influence of God on humankind; her letters (*Briefwechsel*); and her songs (*Lieder*). These four works are the works from which I have compiled the present body which is an attempt to capture Hildegard's images for the first time for English-speaking readers. It is helpful when approaching these writings to take the initial advice of this "prophetissa teutonica" seriously. They are divine inspirations of a highly symbolic nature. They are inspirations that throw themselves upon the mercy of intuitive insight. Our rational "left-brain" age has not been patient or kind to such thinking. We have little time to savor subtle complexities, the nuances seldom are given the space and attention they require to surprise and delight us. We are dared to enjoy the ecstasy of God. And it is never exclusively rational.

These versions have been taken from the German. A concerted effort was made to balance the linguistic demands of English spiritual expression and the integrity of Hildegard's visions.

Be surprised! Allow these renderings of Hildegard's text to lure. For she charges us not only with delight and ecstasy, but also with the co-creative accountability of humankind, a notion most apropos in an age of fomentation such as ours. Hildegard would approve of "fomentation" as an apt description of the human condition and of God. She delights in playing with words in just this way. It may describe, on the one hand, initiation and instigation, and on the other, the therapeutic application of warmth and moisture. This "warm moistness" is her seminal "veriditas", the verdancy, the "greening" power of God. In Hildegard's paradigm, it is the vital force that embraces creation. Without it creation would wither and become arid. This greening power is the pattern for all good. It has its source in God, pouring all fruitfulness, freshness and novelty into creation. Native to a lush Bavarian valley, Hildegard knew of this "veriditas" as a powerful natural force. She perceived how the earth itself "perspired" with this germinating vitality and she applied the observation to humankind.

Yet more than this, she would have us understand that the love between Creator and creature can be compared to the love of husband and wife in vowed fidelity. Creation speaks to the Creator as to a lover and dares to participate in its own co-creation. The implications are clear: Justice for all humankind and Compassion

17

for the earth. If the words are familiar to us today, they are also the same words Hildegard employed on behalf of the earth and persons in her prophetic response to injustice 850 years ago.

...her life.

Hildegard lived in a convent from the time she was eight years old, and reports that even at that young age she experienced God overshadowing her life. Yet it was not until she was forty years old that she began to write down some of the visions and insights she had been gifted with from childhood on. It was through the efforts of Bernard of Clairveaux, whom Hildegard had asked for counsel, that her writings were presented at a Papal Synod in 1147/48.

They were well received and her fame quickly spread. Popes, abbots, emperors, peasants and religious all sought her out for spiritual advice and direction. Hildegard appreciated her role as prophet in the midst of this tumultuous era. Not only was she politically astute, but more importantly, she took her role as spiritual director most seriously—nurturing, disciplining and insisting on justice all in the same breath.

It is of no small significance that her correspondence included excommunicants, many of whom found themselves in that state due to their "poor" politics rather than any lapse in their orthodoxy. She herself, at age 81, was a victim of interdict for purely political reasons. Her last days were spent in a furious exchange of letters to exonerate her name and her abbey, and to see justice done. This being accomplished, she died that same year, 1179, precisely on the date that she had foretold her sisters.

It is significant that Hildegard was part of a curious movement that was afoot in the 12th century. Especially in Germany and the Low Countries, there were brilliant minds critically at work. It was a movement of thoughts that were at once penetrating and spiritual. Delightfully enough, they were women's thoughts. Scholastics and classicists alike have failed to discern the creative bouquet of this vintage nurtured in the Rhine valley. It is only now on what might very well be the crest of a sister movement to that medieval feminist swell, that we find ourselves with palates educated enough to appreciate this spirit. Or is it that the wine served to us til now has run out and suddenly we find that the best has been saved to last? We shall see.

Hildegard wouild have us know God's pleasure. She would have us "meet every creature with grace."

Gabriele Uhlein

GOD:
The Divine

20

A wheel was shone to me,
wonderful to behold...

Divinity is in its omniscience and
 omnipotence
 like a wheel,
  a circle,
  a whole,

 that can neither be understood,
  nor divided,
  nor begun nor ended.

God says:

I am the day unto myself,
not formed by the sun,
but rather,
forming the sun,
igniting it.

I am the understanding not understood,
but rather,
allowing all understanding,
illuminating it.

I have a voice of thunder,
living sound,
the movement of all creatures.

Everlasting Life of life,
I am without beginning,
 without end: God.

I am perpetually stirring and standing,
 always
 at work.

All that God created was already
in God's presence before the world
began,
before the beginning of time.

24

There is
no creation
that does not have a radiance.

>be it greenness or seed,
>blossom or beauty.

It could not be creation without it.

If God had not the power to thus empower,
>the light to thus enlighten,
>where then, would all creation be?

It is easier
to gaze into the sun,
than into the face of the mystery of God.

Such is its beauty and its radiance.

God says:

I am the supreme fire;
not deadly, but rather,
enkindling every spark of life.

I am life, complete unto itself,
    whole,
    sound,
    not needing stones to be sculpted,
    not needing branches to blossom,
    not rooted in human potency.

Rather, all life has its root in me.

Understanding is the root.

The resounding WORD blossoms forth
        from it.

How then,
is it possible for God not to be at work?

God is Understanding.

God put the world together out of
various elements:

> he empowered it with wind,

> he illuminated and connected it
> with stars,

> he filled it with all manner of
> creation.

All this is to the glory of his name.

Who is the Trinity?

You are music.
You are life.

Source of everything,
creator of everything,
angelic hosts sing your praise.

Wonderfully radiant,
deep,
mysterious.

You are alive in everything,
and yet you are unknown to us.

Now here is the image of the power
of God:

This firmanent is an all-encompassing
circle.
No one can say where this wheel begins
or ends.

I, the fiery life of divine wisdom,
I ignite the beauty of the plains,
I sparkle the waters,
I burn in the sun,
      and the moon,
      and the stars.

With wisdom I order ALL rightly.

Above ALL I determine truth.

I am the one whose praise
echoes on high.

I adorn all the earth.

I am the breeze
that nurtures all things
green.
I encourage blossoms to flourish with ripening fruits.

I am led by the spirit to feed
the purest streams.

I am the rain
coming from the dew
that causes the grasses to laugh
with the joy of life.

I call forth tears,
the aroma of holy work.

I am the yearning for good.

Invisible life that sustains ALL,
I awaken to life everything
in every waft of air.

The air is life,
greening and blossoming.

The waters flow with life.

The sun is lit with life.

The moon, when waning, is again
    rekindled by the sun,
        waxing with life once more.

The stars shine,
radiating with life-light.

All creation is gifted with the
ecstasy of God's light.

I govern the light of the skies,
I govern the trees, grasses, and all
    other earthly greenings.

I order the wild creatures,
I order all creeping and crawling things
    over and under the earth.

Who would dare find fault with my
    methods?

In doing good,
the illumination of a good conscience
is like the light of the earthly sun.

If they do not see me in that light,
how can they see me in the dark of
    their hearts?

I am
for all eternity
the vigor of the God-head.

I do not have my source in time.

I am
the divine power
through which God decided and sanctioned
      the creation of all things.

I am
the reflection of providence for all.

I am
the resounding WORD,
the It-Shall-Be
that I intone
with mighty power
from which all the world proceeds.

Thru animate eyes
I divide the seasons
of time.

I am aware of what they are.
I am aware of their potential.

With my mouth
I kiss my own chosen creation

I uniquely,
lovingly,
embrace every image
I have made
out of the earth's clay.

With a fiery spirit
I transform it
into a body
to serve
all the world.

Just as a circle embraces all that
is within it,
so does the God-head embrace all.

No one has the power to divide this
circle,
to surpass it,
or to limit it.

Who is the Holy Spirit?
The Holy Spirit is a Burning Spirit.
It kindles
the hearts of humankind.
Like tympanum and lyre it plays them,
gathering volume in the temple of the soul.

Holy Spirit is
Life-giving-life,
all movement.

Root of all being.

Purifier of all impurity.

Absolver of all faults.

Balm of all wounds.

Radiant life, worthy of all praise,
The Holy Spirit resurrects and awakens
everything that is.

Truly,
the Holy Spirit is an unquenchable fire.

He bestows all excellence,
    sparks all worth,
    awakes all goodness,
    ignites speech,
    enflames humankind.

Yet in this radiance is a restorative
                stillness.
It is the stillness that is similarly
in the will to good.
It spreads to all sides.

The Holy Spirit, then,
through one's fervent longings,
pours the juice of contrition
into the hardened human heart.

Holy Spirit,
All creation praises you.
Creation has life because of you.
You are precious salve for broken bones,
　　　　　for festering wounds.
You transform them to precious gems.
Now gather us together in your praise.
Lead us on the proper path.

　　In the aimless, spinning soul
　　where fog obscures the intellect and will,
　　where the fruit is noxious and poisonous,
　　you guide the pruning sword.

　　Thus the spirit orders all desire.

　　But should the soul
　　incline to be coveteous and incorrigible,
　　fixing its gaze on evil's face,
　　looking ever with eyes of malice,
　　you rush in with fire,
　　and burn,
　　as you will.

O Holy Spirit,
Fiery Comforter Spirit
Life of the life of all creatures,

Holy are you,
    you that give existence
    to all form.

Holy are you,
    you that are balm for the
    mortally wounded.

Holy are you,
    you that cleanse deep hurt.

Fire of love,
breath of all holiness,
you are so delicious to our hearts.

You infuse our hearts deeply with
the good smell of virtue.

O Holy Spirit,

Clear fountain,
in you we perceive God,
how he gathers the perplexed
and seeks the lost.

Bulwark of life,
you are the hope of oneness for that which
is separate.

You are the girdle of propriety,
you are holy salvation.

Shelter those caught in evil,
free those in bondage,
for the divine power wills it.

You are the mighty way in which every
thing that is in the heavens,
on the earth,
and under the earth,
is penetrated with connectedness,
is penetrated with relatedness.

Holy Spirit,

Through you
    clouds billow,
    breezes blow,
    stones drip with trickling streams,
       streams that are the source
       of earth's lush greening.

Likewise,
you are the source of human understanding.

You bless with the breath of wisdom.

Thus all of our praise is yours,
you who are the melody itself of praise,
       the joy of life,
       the mighty honor,
       the hope
    of those to whom you give the gifts
    of the light.

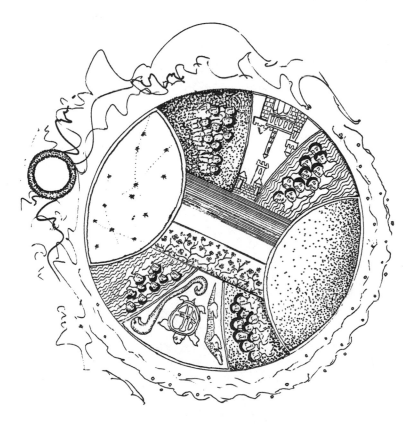

COSMOS:

The Manifestation of God

44

Glance at the sun.

See the moon and the stars.

Gaze at the beauty of earth's greenings.

Now,
think.

What delight
God gives
to humankind
with all these things.

Who gives all these shining, wonderful
gifts, if not God?

Humankind should ponder God...
recognize God's wonders and signs.

Let these signs and wonders be
the firmament on which to build,
  so as not to be shaken by fear,
  or distracted from the love
  of God.

The blowing wind,
the mild, moist air,
the exquisite greening
of trees and grasses —

In their beginning,

in their ending,

they give God their praise.

The air,
blowing everywhere
serves all creatures.

Ever is the firmament its support.

Ever is it held,
carried,
by the power of God.

Without the WORD of God
no creature has being.

God's WORD is in all creation,
visible and invisible.

The WORD
is living,
being,
spirit,
all verdant greening,
all creativity.

All creation
is awakened,
called,
by the resounding melody,
God's invocation of the WORD.

This WORD manifests in every creature.

Now this is how the spirit is in the
flesh — the WORD is indivisible from GOD.

God is the foundation
for everything.

This God undertakes,
God gives,

Such that nothing
that is necessary
for life
is lacking.

Now humankind needs a body
that at all times
honors and praises God.

This body is supported in every way
through the earth.

Thus the earth glorifies the power
of God.

As the creator loves his creation,
so creation loves the Creator.

Creation,
of course,
was fashioned to be adorned,
    to be showered,
    to be gifted with the love of
        the Creator.

The entire world has been embraced
by this kiss.

God has gifted creation with everything
that is necessary.

Limitless love,
from the depths to the stars:
    flooding all,
    loving all.

It is the royal kiss of peace.

The sun is set in the firmament of
heaven.
It watches over earthly creation,
letting nothing perish.

God watches over us in just such a way.

In no way,
can a believer that sets
heart and being on God,
ever be forgotten by God.

The sun climbs in its course
and at mid-day burns in full glow.

This is how it is with those who
                    are just.

They demonstrate fullness and justice.
They cannot be hindered,
just as the sun cannot be hindered
        in its ascent.

No warmth ever goes to waste.

The earth is to the sun,
as the soul is to God.

The earth,
at any point,
can be located by its relationship
        to the sun.

The earth has a scaffold of stones and
trees. In the same way is a person formed:
        flesh is the earth,
        the bones are the trees and stones.

The soul is the firmament of the organism,
then.
In the manner in which the soul permeates
the body with its energy, it causes and
consummates all human action.

This is how a person becomes a flowering
        orchard.

The person that does good works is indeed
this orchard bearing good fruit. And this
is just like the earth with its ornamentation
of stone and blossoming trees.

In all that the earth issues forth from God,
    it is connected and bound to God.

Nothing can be undertaken without
God's bidding.

It is just like the wife
gazing at her husband
to do his bidding and desire.

In just such a way
creation feels drawn to her creator
as she responds to him in service.

But the creator, too,
is bound to creation.

He showers upon it greening refreshment,
the vitality to bear fruit.

I compare
the great love
of Creator and creation
to the same love and fidelity
with which God
binds woman and man
together.

This is so
that together
they might be creatively fruitful.

Creation
is allowed
in intimate love,
to speak
to the Creator
as if to a lover.

Creation
is allowed
to ask
for a pasture,
a homeland.

Out of the Creator's fullness,
this request is granted to creation.

The earth is at the same time
mother,
she is mother of all that is natural,
    mother of all that is human.

She is the mother of all,
for contained in her
are the seeds of all.

The earth of humankind
contains all moistness,
    all verdancy,
    all germinating power.

It is in so many ways
fruitful.
All creation comes from it.
Yet it forms not only the basic
raw material for humankind,
but also the substance
of the incarnation
of God's son.

Flowing in and out like the breath,
the marrow of the hip sweats its essence,
carrying and strengthening the person.
In just such a manner
the vitality of earth's elements
comes from the strength of the creator.

It is this vigor that hugs the world:
warming, moistening, firming, greening.

This is so that all creatures
might germinate and grow.

When in the fullness of its time
this creation wilts,
its vigor returns to its own source.

This is the underlying natural law.
When the elements of the world fulfill
their function,
they come to ripeness
and their fruit is gathered back to God.

Now these things
are in reference to the soul's life:
spiritual vitality is alive in the soul
in the same way as the marrow of the
          hips in the flesh.

Out of the soul in good standing,
the vigor of the virtues flows out
as do the elements of creation,
it flows back in the same capacity
in attentive prayer.

The soul is a breath of living spirit,
that with excellent sensitivity,
permeates the entire body to give it life.

Just so,
the breath of the air makes the earth
fruitful.

Thus the air is the soul of the earth,
moistening it,
greening it.

When a forest does not green vigorously,
then it is no longer a forest.

When a tree does not blossom,
it can not bear fruit.

Likewise a person can not be fruitful
without the greening power of faith,
and an understanding of scripture.

The soul that is full of wisdom
is saturated with the spray of
a bubbling fountain — God himself.

Holy persons draw to themselves
all that is earthly.

God has arranged all things in the world
in consideration of everything else.

The more one learns about that
which one knows nothing of,
the more one gains in wisdom.
One has, therefore,
through science,
eyes with which it behooves us
to pay attention.

Creation would become totally black
if in any way
the Godly command is shirked.

Creation blooms and flourishes
when it remains in right relationship
and keeps to its assigned tasks.

Creation is to serve humankind
in its bodily needs,
and to be for the health of the soul
as well.

The air,
with its penetrating strength,
characterizes
the victorious banner that is trust.

It gives light
to the fire's flame
and sprinkles
the imagination of believers
with the dew of hope.

Thus does trust show the way.

Those who breathe this dew
long for heavenly things.
They carry within
  refreshing,
  fulfilling,
  greening love,
with which they hasten to the aid of all.

With the passion of heavenly yearning,
they produce rich fruit.

Like billowing clouds,
like the incessant gurgle of the brook,
the longing of the soul can never be
stilled.

It is this longing with which holy
persons seek their work from God.

All nature is at the disposal of
humankind.
We are to work with it.

Without it we can not survive.

In the world,
it is possible for a person to do
either good or bad.

As a result of the latter,
a body is placed in many afflictions.
To lessen them,
a person should therefore
act according to the judgement of a
      spiritual director,
lest one find only the bitterness
and not the sweetness of life.

Believing persons
should never cease
to direct themselves and others
to God.

This is so that God,
seeing the hearts of humankind,
might make return
for just work and good will.

To a person of good will,
God will grant what is asked,
as the will to good
is the sweetest of all aromas.

Already under the old covenant
God was less pleased
with the blood of rams,
but rather
delighted in the goodwill of humankind.

When one's thoughts
are neither frivolous nor flippant,

when one's thoughts
are neither stiff-necked nor stupid,

but rather,
are harmonious —

they habitually
render
physical calm
and deep insight.

Envy drives out all greening power!

When the greedy do not get
what they want,
they fall into a depression
from which they are not lightly lifted.

The day hurries quickly by,
They say, "it is always night."

If happiness should stand outside,
just beyond their door,
they say, "I am accursed."

Should it go well
with all they undertake,
still they would say, "it goes badly!"

You snakelike, hellish tongues!
You dare to live without
the verdancy of God's grace.

Thus,
Humankind does well to keep honesty,
   to keep to truth.

Those that love lies
bring suffering
not only to themselves
but to others as well,
since they are driven to ever more lies.

These lies are like juiceless foam,
            hard and black.
Lacking the verdancy of justice,
it is dry,
totally without tender goodness,
totally without illuminating virtue.

Now in the people
that were meant to green,
there is no more life of any kind.
There is only shrivelled barrenness.

The winds are burdened
by the utterly awful stink of evil,
selfish goings-on.

Thunderstorms menace.

The air belches out
the filthy uncleanliness of the peoples.

There pours forth an unnatural,
a loathsome darkness,
that withers the green,
and wizens the fruit
that was to serve as food for the people.

Sometimes this layer of air
is full,
full of a fog that is the source
of many destructive and barren creatures,
that destroy and damage the earth,
rendering it incapable
of sustaining humanity.

God desires
that all the world
be pure in his sight.

The earth should not be injured.
The earth should not be destroyed.

As often as the elements,
the elements of the world
are violated
by ill-treatment,
so God will cleanse them.

God will cleanse them
thru the sufferings,
thru the hardships
of humankind.

The high,
the low,
all of creation,
God gives to humankind to use.

If this privilege is misused,
God's Justice permits creation to
punish humanity.

HUMANKIND:

CO—Creators of Divine
Manifestation

Through this world God encircles
and strengthens humankind.

Through and through, great power is
ours,
such that
all creation,
in all things,
stands by us.

Just like the fishes
that dance
in the waters of trust,

God feeds
the contrite
with nourishment
of life.

He permeates
humankind
with his issue.

How wonderful
is the wisdom
in the God-head's heart.

It is the heart that sees
the primordial eternity
of every creature.

When God gazes upon the countenance
of humankind,
the face that he formed,
he contemplates this work
in its totality,
its totality in this human form.

How wonderful is this breath then,
this breath that awakened humankind.

Elemental power of eternity,
in your heart you order all things.

Everything is created,
as you will it,
through your word.

And this,
your WORD,
took on flesh in Adam's form.

Thus much painful suffering is taken from
this form.

Humanity finds itself in the midst
of the world.

In the midst of all other creatures
humanity is the most significant
and yet the most dependent upon
the others.

Humanity is small in stature,
but powerful in strength of soul.

With head directed upward,
with feet on firm ground,
humanity can set all things in motion,
      things above as well as
      things below.

The human person
is the form
and the fullness
of creation.

In humankind,
God brings to fullness all his creation.

God created humankind,
so that humankind
might cultivate the earthly
and thereby
create the heavenly.

Humankind
should be the banner of divinity.

Divinity

is aimed

at humanity.

Good People,

Most royal greening verdancy,
rooted in the sun,
you shine with radiant light.

In this circle of earthly existence
you shine
so finely,
it surpasses understanding.

God hugs you.
You are encircled
by the arms
of the mystery of God.

And as human persons view creation
  with compassion,
  in trust,
they see the Lord.

It is God which humankind is then
able to recognize in every living
thing.

Does not humanity know that God
is the world's creator?

Just as it occurred to God to create
  humankind,
so it occurs to God to save those that
  trust
  in him.

The soul is kissed by God
in its innermost regions.

With interior yearning,
grace and blessing
are bestowed.

It is a yearning to take on God's
    gentle yoke,
it is a yearning to give one's self
    to God's way.

The marvels of God
are not brought forth
from one's self.

Rather,
it is more like a chord,
a sound that is played.

The tone does not come
out of the chord itself,
but rather,
thru the touch
of the musician.

I am, of course,
the lyre and harp
of God's kindness.

God says:
>   Ever

>   you are

>   before my eyes.

God, I am your opus.

Before the beginnning of time,
already then,
I was in your mind.

God has created me.
God is my Lord,
>   having dominion over me.

God is also my strength,
>   for I can wish to do nothing
>   good without God.

Thru God I have living spirit.
Thru God I have life and movement.
Thru God I learn, I find my path.

If I call in truth, this God and
Lord directs my steps;
setting my feet to the rhythm of
his precepts.

I run like a deer that seeks its
>   spring.

I have my home on high,
I meet every creature of the world
with grace.

I am the life and verdancy of good works.
I am the yoke of all virtue.

I am the delight and illumination
        of love of God,
    the form of all seeking for him.

All that God wills, I will.

With wings of good intention,
I fly the dome of the sky
to accomplish the will of God in all.

And so I climb ever higher...
to where I see God's doings
face to face.

Now I seek no more,
desire no more,
wish no more but what is holy.

Thus,
I am in every respect,
of a heavenly nature.

Under your protection,
I rejoice, O God!

In your shadow,
I exult, O God!

You rescue me from the heaviness of sin.

My soul anticipates
drawing ever closer to you
in the doing of good works.

This supreme longing
pulls me to you,
beckons me come
under your protection,
into the shadow of your power.

I am secure from all enemies there!

Show yourself to me
in the beauty of your precepts
so that I might
with all my love
hold you fast in my soul.

Incarnating,
you have redeemed me;
dying,
you have awakened me.

Now you have brought all your work
to fullness —
in virgin nature you found pasture,
in virgin nature you assumed flesh.

Now it came to pass that man lacked
a help-mate that was his equal.

God created this help-mate in the form
of a woman — a mirror image of all that
was latent in the male sex.

In this way, man and woman are so
intimately related that one is the
work of the other.

Man can not be called man without woman.
Neither can woman be named woman without
man.

The woman is the labor of the man.
The man is an aspect of comfort for the woman.

One does not have the capacity of living without the other.

Man is an allusion to the divinity of
the God-head; woman is a reference to the
humanity of the Son of God.

Thus,
humankind, man and woman,
is enthroned over creation
and all creatures are in the care of
        men and women.

Humankind,
in this way,
is more than creation.

It is the guardian of creation.

In Nature, God established humankind
in power.

We are dressed in the scaffold of
creation:
in seeing — to recognize
all the world,
in hearing — to understand,
in smelling — to discern,
in tasting — to nurture,
in touching — to govern.
In this way humankind comes to know God,
for God is the author of all creation.

Now God has built the human form into the world structure, indeed even the cosmos, just as an artist would use a particular pattern in her work.

God be praised in his handiwork:
Humankind.

And so,
humankind
full of all creative possibilities,
is God's work.

Humankind alone,
is called to assist God.

Humankind is called to co-create.

With nature's help,
humankind can set into creation
all that is necessary and life sustaining.

God's majesty is glorified
in the manifestation of every manner
      of nature's fruitfulness.

This is possible,
possible through the right and holy
      utilization of the earth,
the earth in which humankind has its
      source.

The sum total of heaven and earth,
everything in nature,
is thus won to use and purpose.

It becomes a temple and altar
for the service of God.

In serving God,
humankind is much loved
by him.

God is delighted by humankind.

Indeed,
God himself
has created humankind
and given it all worth.

God allows himself to be disturbed
by it!

God says:

> In the shaking out of my mantle
> you are drenched,
> watered,
> with thousands upon thousands
> of drops
> of precious dew.

Thus is humanity gifted.

Yet when I say that this and this is so,
it is not brought about
by a gentle and unobtrusive
WORD.

If the earth is constantly being softened
by rain and fertilizer,
if it has no hardness,
it can not bear fruit.

Nothing ever ripens
under such conditions.
There would be only mush and floods.

I have been moved by the form of
humankind.

I have kissed it,
grounding it
in faithful relationship.

Thus,
I have exalted humankind
with the vocation of creation.

I call humankind to the same norm.

Humankind demonstrates two aspects:
    the singing of praise to God,
    and the doing of good works.

God is made known through praise,
And in good works
    the wonders of God can be seen.

In the praise of God
a person is like an angel.
But it is the doing of good works
that is the hallmark of humanity.

This completeness
makes humankind the fullest creation
            of God.

It is in praise and service
that the surprise of God is consummated.

The work of God,
God brings to fullness in humankind.

Humankind:
      Fashioned in God's image and in
         God's likeness,
      inscribed in God's every
         creation,
      forever in the plan of God,
      the completion of his work.

This work's consummation
is the giving to humankind
the entire creation,

that men and women might work it to fullness
in the self-same manner in which
God imaged humankind.

The human
is the very garment
with which my Son robed himself
in royal splendor,
showed himself
as God of all creation
and Life of all life.

Now this human is rightly called "alive",
because as long as the person exists
on the breath of the Holy Spirit,
the person is indeed, life.

While humankind
was being beguiled
by the advice of the snake,

I made my passionate appearance.

In the enkindled womb of the virgin
I came to rest.
I became human in her flesh.

After I came forth
from the virgin's womb,
I brought humankind home again
in the waters of baptism
through which I purified
the human seed.

Mary,
ground of all being,
Greetings!

Greetings to you, lovely and loving Mother!
You birthed to earth your son,
You birthed the son of God from heaven
      by breathing the spirit of God.

Mary,

The heavens
gift the grass
with moist dew.

The entire earth
rejoices.

From your womb
the seed
sprouted forth.

The birds of the air
nest
in this tree.

Blessed is the fruit of your womb!

Your womb's fruitfulness
is food for humankind.

Great is the joy
at this delicious banquet!

In you,
mild virgin,
is the fullness of all joy.

Mary,

O luminous mother,
holy, healing art!

Eve brought sorrow to the soul
but by your holy son
you pour balm
on death's wounds and travail.

You have indeed conquered death!

You have established life!

Ask for us life.
Ask for us radiant joy.

Ask for us the sweet, delicious ecstasy
  that is forever yours.

Mary,

God delights in you so much,
God was so taken with you,
    he sank his love's fire
    deep within you.

So much love he gave you,
    that with it you nurture his son.

So full of ecstasy is your body
that it resounds with heaven's symphony.

Your womb exults.

It exults like the grass,
    grass the dew has nestled on,
    grass the dew has infused with
        verdant strength.

That is how it is with you,
Mother of all joy.

A SONG TO MARY:

You glowing,
most green,
verdant sprout,

in the movement of the spirit,
in the midst of wise and holy seekers,
you bud forth into light.

Your time to blossom had come.

Balsam scented,
in you
the beautiful flower
blossomed.

It is the beautiful flower
that lends its scent
to those herbs,
all that had shrivelled and wilted.

It brings them
lush greenness
once more.

It is through water
that the Holy Spirit
overcomes
all injustice,
bringing to fulfillment
all his gifts...

gifts,
such that
humankind might thrive
in the moisture of justice
and stream to spiritual things
in the current of truth.

Has humankind never discovered God
on the path of justice?

Have people never observed
how the earthly seed comes to growth
when it falls to the ground
and is soaked by rain and dew?

As if this could come to pass
thru any other
than the creator of all things!

Gazing at God then,
they would forget all evil,
just like a person
cannot remember how they were born,
even though they know
that they were indeed born.

122

When a person understands Justice
the self is let go.

The just taste and drink virtue.
This strengthens them, as if
they were addicted to wine,
yet they are never beside
themselves,
are never uncontrollable,
or know not what they do,
as is the case with drunkards.

The just love God,
of whom there can be no surfeit,
only utter, constant ecstasy.

The first seed of the longing for Justice
blows through the soul like the wind.

The taste for good will plays in it
like a breeze.

The consummation of this seed
is a greening in the soul
that is like that
of the ripening world.

Now the soul honors God
by the doing of just deeds.

The soul is only as strong as its works.

Just as the creation of God,
that is, humankind,
never ceases to come to an end,
but rather, continually develops,
so also the works of humankind
shall not disappear.

Those things that tend toward God
shall shine forth in the heavens,
while those that are devilish
shall become notorious through their
ill effects.

God gave to humankind the talent
to create with all the world.

Just as the person shall never end,
until into dust they are transformed
        and resurrected,
just so,
their works are always visible.

The good deeds shall glorify,
the bad deeds shall shame,
insofar as they have not been blotted out
        through penance.

Who are the prophets?
They are a royal people,
who penetrate mystery
and see with the spirit's eyes.

In illuminating darkness they speak out.

They are living, penetrating clarity.
They are a blossom blooming only
on the shoot that is rooted in the
flood of light.

I saw a mighty and immeasurable
      marvelousness.

It had such a fierce shine
I could only behold it
as if through a mirror.

But I knew that within it
was every manner of sweet blossoming,
      every manner of good aromas and
          lovely scents.
It was to be enjoyed
with unbounded delight.

Here were the blessed, happy ones
that moved God in their time on earth,
stirred God with sincere striving and
      just works.

Now in all this marvelousness
they can enjoy the sweetest ecstasy.

Be not lax
in celebrating,
Be not lazy
in the festive service of God.

Be ablaze with enthusiasm.
Let us be an alive,
burning offering
before the altar of God!

The Mystics are for Everyone

Some reflections by Matt Fox on the

Meditations with ™
Series

Because I have been scandalized by the ignorance of and lack of appreciation of Western Mystics by Westerners, I have worked with Bear & Company to create the Meditations With Series.

Thomas Merton used to tell the story of how Buddhist Doctor Suzuki "forced" him into reading Meister Eckhart, "the greatest mystic of the Western church." Whole monasteries and convents of Benedictine monks and nuns no longer know St. Hildegarde of Bingen, osb. Dominicans have become Thomists rather than lively "livers" of Aquinas' daring visions like Eckhart was. Academicians translate and footnote the mystics and thus reduce their "juiciness" (Hildegarde's word) to the dry rot apolitical and sexist violence of their own privileged positions.

The result of all this the young are driven East. Workers of social justice burn out. Liturgy grows stale. Society grows cynical.

This series presents the mystics with respect for their prophetic challenge and our hungry imaginations.

We need the mystics. We need our own Western mystics. We have a right to them. The Meditations With Series will enable us to get our mystics off the shelves and into the guts and hearts of people who want to live deeply.

The Meditations With Series offers reliable "versions" in highly readable formats with attractive art suitable for these great artists of the Spirit.

Meditations

WITH ™

Meister Eckhart

a centering book by
MATT FOX

Eckhart was no closet monk. This book shares his words and the tradition that believes that life itself—living and dying, growing and sinning, groaning and celebrating—is the creative energy of God.

For the first time the writings of this great mystic, prophet, feminist, philosopher, preacher and theologian, administrator and poet, spiritual genius and once declared heretic collected and edited in this treasury of inspiration.

WHERE SHOULD WE BEGIN?

Begin with the heart. For the spring of Life arises from the heart and from there it runs in a circular manner. For Eckhart to be spiritual is to be awake and alive—Creation itself is a sacrament. The spiritual life begins where life does—"the spring of life" or the heart.

Reflections of Meister Eckhart with an introduction by MATT FOX based in the tradition that spirituality begins with humanity's potential to act divinely in the ways of beauty-making compassion. and sharing.

The basics of Eckhart made simple—the principles and writings arranged for meditation and learning. Perfect for day by day readings and meditations.

A perfect gift.   paper
ca. 128 pages
ISBN: 0-939680-04-1

Meditations WITH™

Mechtild of Magdeburg
a centering book by Sue Woodruff

Mechtild of Magdeburg, a 13th century woman-mystic left behind one book which is a spiritual journey. From this book, *Flowing Light of the Godhead*, Sue Woodruff gleans poignant versions.

Like so many women of the middle ages she was a prophet who loudly decried the abuses of organized religions and its priests in her day. While she made enemies this way, she did not cease composing this beautiful poetry of a soul nor did she stop her spiritual life very much grounded in the world and the activities of everyday life.

Sue Woodruff brings together, in moving drawings, and well chosen verse from Mechtild, a beautiful meditation experience— one based on God's beautiful creation, and humanity's dignity in God.
ISBN 0-939680-04-1   128 pages

Meditations WITH™

Julian of Norwich
a centering book by Brendan Doyle

"The first English woman of Letters," Julian of Norwich, the 14th century mystic stressed the goodness of creation and emphasized the compassion and reverence that God has for each creature. Her emphasis on God's personal love for creatures unwittingly weakened the spirit of legalism which was providing a sense of security for the established leadership.

Despite her uncompromising convictions, Julian's anthropology and theology maintain an affirmative tone. This positive thrust is rooted in her understanding of creation as a self-revelation of the Creator. Her anthropology emerges from the creature's fundamental relationship with its maker. She emphasized the enduring nature of this primary relationship by noting that anyone who loves creatures into being certainly intends to care for them and provide for their needs, whatever they may be. Perhaps this is why Julian is at ease with the Motherhood AND Fatherhood of the God Spirit.

Twentieth century men and women who are seeking the same peace and security that their fourteenth century counterparts desired can discover the same sense of affirmation and acceptance in the knowledge that God loves them, too, and desires to share a life of intimate communion with them. Julian's teaching promises today's men and women the opportunity to re-shape their perception of everyday life.

ISBN 0-939680-11-4   128 pages

ORIGINAL BLESSING

The basics of a wholistic healing spirituality with nature.

—a primer in creation spirituality
By MATT FOX

This book by MATT FOX, outlining the main themes of the spiritual journey of the Creation-Centered Spiritual traditions, has been years in the making.

Writing in the simple, fluid style that has made MATT FOX a best-selling author for years, the author lays out in a clear and definitive way the priniciple elements in the creation traditions. This tradition is the oldest in the western scriptures being based not in "original sin" theologies but with ORIGINAL BLESSING—How are we, and how is creation, an ORIGINAL BLESSING, meant to bless and not curse creation and one another? What are the implications of a spirituality oriented to Cosmic living rather than to introspective guilty conscience?

ISBN 0-939680-07-6   264 pages

WHEE! We, wee All the Way Home ..

A GUIDE TO A SENSUAL PROPHETIC SPIRITUALITY.

Back in print with a completely new *Foreword to the 80s* by Matthew Fox.

"This book has excitement, color, swiftness and is service to the Church. WHEE! is a book for searchers into the meaning of life and revelation." *Review for Religious*

"WHEE! is provocative, exciting, and radical both in its scope and ideas. It is both socially relevant and psychologically sound."
Library Journal

"This is a pioneer book . . . a voyage replete with new ideas and seldom seen perspectives."
Thomasa F. O'Meara

"Constructive, humane, and joyful in its positive suggestions to improve life quality in a dangerously jaded world." Daniel Turner, National Association of Family Therapists and Counsellors.

264 pages   paper
ISBN: 0-938680-00-9

*All Spirituality is about roots.
For all spirituality is about living..*

WESTERN SPIRITUALITY

Historical Roots, Ecumenical Routes

by Matthew Fox

Now in its third printing!

Matthew Fox has brought together 17 readable scholars to explore a neglected tradition of western spirituality that emphasizes humanity's divinization rather than its fall.

The New Review of Books and Religion calls the volume: "an exciting and important book . . . a pleasant alternative to the oppressive burden of the fall/redemption tradition."

Nicolas Berdyaev, Rosemary Ruether, M.D. Chenu and Jon Sobrin are among those who explore the historical roots of the tradition.

In part two scholars from a variety of traditions provide insights into various forms of the spiritual journey today. Mary Jose Hobday, Monika Hellwig, Justin O'Brien and Richard Woods are among the writers in this section.

The first edition of this book sold out within months and is now available exclusively from *Bear & Company*.

440 pages
ISBN: 0-939680-01-7

"Challenging, exciting presenta-
tion of penetrating insights into
the spirituality of Luke and its
relevance today."

LUKE
SPIRITUALITY

by Leonard Doohan, Ph.D.
Chairperson, Religious Studies, Gonzaga University

This thorough and highly readable treat-
ment of the writing of Luke-Acts demonstrates
the vital and delicate relationship between
spirituality and scripture as seen in Luke—*a
tool to integrate the past of Jesus with the
today of the Christian.*

Dr. Doohan demonstrates how the Lucan
writers tell of the success of the Christian life
as living in the now. Luke is seen as both aware
of the cultural times and the timelessness of his
message.

In Luke the Christian life is developed as a
life of letting go. Luke the spiritual master
promises spiritual success no matter how
circuitous the route we take.

*"thorough, coherent, comprehensive, scho-
larly...but not pedantic."*

CONTENT: New Testament Spirituality,
model Christian, sources of faith, *theology of
ministry*, images of God, *church and life*, call of
discipleship, *universal concerns*, Luke-Acts
spirituality today, *studies on Luke Acts*.

400 pages   paper
ISBN: 0-939680-03-3

Symbion

Spirituality for a possible future
by Richard Woods

A daring series of explorations in spirituality as a way toward a possibly better future......
problems and promises... trends already bearing us along startling trajectories...

ON PROJECT EARTH—Unless we drastically and quickly change our priorities concerning the earth and its fragile, interconnecting ecosystems, we may well live to see the wholesale destruction of this, our only home.

ON ENVIROMENTAL SPIRITUALITY—Our present crisis is total because it is enviromental, affecting every aspect of our life on this planet. A Spirituality for the future must necessarily be enviromental.

ON THE FUTURE OF STRESS— Stress, as a psychosomatic response to life-events, is a spiritual concern as much as it is an issue for physical and mental health.

ISBN 0-939680-08-4   264 pages

"This book contains much practical information."
Elisabeth Kubler-Ross
HOSPICE:
a handbook for families and others facing terminal illness
By James Ewens and Patricia Herrington
of the Milwaukee Hopsice

"One of the greatest contributions that this book will make is to help families know that it is possible to care for a dying loved one at home if hospice care is available. Thus, terminal illness no longer means dying in an institution where the patient is isolated from those he loves at a time when he/she needs to be with them most. Hospice provides an alternative way of caring for the dying."

Josefina B. Magno, M.D.
Executive Director   National Hospice Organization

Hospice: a handbook for families and others

Sections include: "FAMILY; Questions on Hospice Care; REFLECTIONS FROM FAMILIES; Helping Children; SUPPORT SYSTEMS; Legal Considerations; FUNERAL ARRANGEMENTS; Aspects of Grieving; SPIRITUAL CARE; AND, Information for Hospices.

ISBN 0-939680-10-6   244 pages, photography

TAPES BY MATTHEW FOX AND FRIENDS

One of the country's most popular retreat masters and spiritual guides has prepared an extraordinary cassette program.

+ MATTHEW FOX has prepared 15 complete tape programs rooted in a vision of a prayer life that has its flower in compassionate caring.

+ Jose Hobday, Msgr Robert Fox, Brian Swimme, MATT and other friends share their experience, strength and hope with you.

+ Spend a weekend with them . . . stretch them over days or weeks

+ Use them at home . . . lone, in a group . . . in a classroom, or in your car.

+ A fresh, imaginative, prayer resource you've been waiting for.

JUST RELEASED!

TAPE 15: Spirituality and Education
In this tape Matt Fox shares his insights into a Creation-Centered approach to education. He draws from his experiences as teacher/learner. He discounts the "Jacob's ladder approach to education as doing something to another or superior/inferior relationships. He demonstrates concrete ways in which teachers and "students" can dance "Sarah's Circle" of compassion, caring, wisdom and inter-dependence. The discipline of reverencing life constitutes the heart of all human learning.

TAPE 14: Science, Spirituality and Education
Matt Fox dialogues with physicist/mathematician Dr. Brian Swimme in exploring the connection between the Mysteries of the Universe and Our Christian Spirituality. They describe their MANIFESTO (see this catalogue) for a global community. A renewed spirituality will allow a dialogue of science, education, and culture if religious faith will not seek its own perpetuation but will believe deeply enough that it can let go of its own privileged positions in order to be among the least and the poorest.

TAPE EIGHT: Holiness as Cosmic Hospitality
Pointing out that the meaning of holiness must be sought for our time. The theological explanation of hospitality, God as host/hostess, and the practical ramifications of hospitality to *self, others, nature* and *God.*

TAPE SEVEN: Images of Soul: psychology of spirituality
A terminal case of "left-brain-itis" haunts western civilization. Words have lost their moorings and meanings. Philosopher Charles Fair points out that when a civilization looses its meaning of "soul" that civilization dies. Today, in the west, we have lost the meaning of soul and we need to return to "right-brain" insights for soul. These are expressed by images—out of new images of soul a new civilization can be born. Special attention is given to Meister Eckhart's images of soul.

TAPE SIX: Recovering Ritual in the West: liturgy & spirituality
A look at liturgy, music and ritual. An analysis of what's wrong in the west plus antidotes for healing. This analysis includes the absence of cosmos, body, social justice, and via negativa when westerners gather to worship. Antidotes for healing this malaise are noted with special attention paid to the prophetic role of music.

TAPE 13: Body as Metaphor

Jungian Analyst John Giannini and Matt Fox discuss the recovery of the holy trinity of Body, Soul, and Spirit. Eckhardt's wholistic, cosmic spirituality and Jung's principle of synchronicity heal the microcosm and macrocosm of western consciousness torn asunder by an ascetic dualism that pits spirit against matter.

TAPE 12: Creativity & Spirituality— a trialogue with Jose Hobday, Msgr. Robert Fox, and Matthew Fox.

Street Priest, Msgr. Robert Fox of Harlem shares his experience of a creation-centered spirituality on the streets of New York. All three share that finding God in the midst of life is finding yourself, your neighbor, and all of creation and believing "it is good."

TAPE 11: An American Spirituality

Matt Fox believes that the phenomenon of prayer and interest in adult spirituality is clearly at the forefront of American culture today. In this tape he presents the forms this phenommenon takes and some of the reasons "why" we should not be surprised. Prayer as a cover up for injustice is dead. The quest of the American spirituality may be to end the CHAOS.

TAPE 10: A Native American Spirituality

Native American, Sister Jose Hobday dialogues with Matt Fox regarding the creation-centered tradition of the Native American Spirituality. Explored are images of soul, community, and person.

TAPE NINE: Social Justice, Art & Spirituality: a Holy Trinity and indivisible unity

Part and parcel of every unjust system is the separation of justice and art. Such separation renders art as mere entertainment or as investment for the powerful. Yet art remains the meaningful link between theory and social change; and between personal transformation & social transformation. This tape explores bringing the trinity of social justice, art and spirituality together again.

TAPE FIVE: Pleasure, Contemplation | Social Justice: antidote to the idolatry of consumeri...

This meaning of contemplation as pleasure and savoring contemplation. This meaning of contemplation as pleasure and savoring contemplation . . . One reason why consumerism has taken such deep root in western culture is that western spiritualities have too often ignored a theology of pleasure. The Holy Spirit is discovered as the "Spirit of Transformation."

TAPE FOUR: Images of Compassion: East meets West

It seems that when you get to the roots of all major world spiritual traditions, they are all trying to teach people compassion. This tape examines four images found in all world religions to educate in compassion.

TAPE THREE: Psychology & Mysticism—Jung & Meister Eckhart

Jung admits his dependence on the great Dominican mystic Meister Eckhart when he writes that reading Meister Eckhart gave him "the key" to opening up the unconscious. This tape examines the insights into the human spirit uncovered by Meister Eckhart and Carl Gustave Jung; the importance of matter in our spiritual life.

TAPE TWO: Family Spirituality

The 1980's have been declared the decade of the family. This reflection considers three dimensions to family and spirituality: 1) The meaning of family with special attention to the cosmic family or "family of being" of which biblical tradition teaches; 2) Our family or local unit of intimacy as mystical energy source—family as celebration; and 3) Our family or local unit of intimacy as a prophetic energy—the family as a resistance unit.

TAPE ONE: From Climbing Jacob's Ladder to Dancing Sarah's Circle

A reflection on the change in mystical symbols from the overly competitive and self-centered "climbing Jacob's ladder" to the symbol of interdependence, creativity, humor and gentle living characterized by "Sarah's Circle."

Qty	ORDER FORM	Each	Total
	Bear & Company "little magazine"	**$30.00 yr.**	
	CANADIAN ORDERS: ADD $6.00 FOR PROCESSING		
	TAPE ONE: Climbing/Dancing	7.95	
	TAPE TWO: Family Spirituality	7.95	
	TAPE THREE: Psychology & Mysticism	7.95	
	TAPE FOUR: Images of Compassion	7.95	
	TAPE FIVE: Pleasure, Contemplation, Justice	7.95	
	TAPE SIX: Recovering Ritual	7.95	
	TAPE SEVEN: Images of Soul	7.95	
	TAPE EIGHT: Holiness Cosmic Hospitality	7.95	
	TAPE NINE: Social Justice, ART, Spirituality	7.95	
	TAPE 10: A Native American Spirituality	7.95	
	TAPE 11: An American Spirituality	7.95	
	TAPE 12: A Spirituality for the Streets	7.95	
	TAPE 13: Body as Metaphor	7.95	
	TAPE 14: Science, Spirituality & Education	7.95	
	TAPE 15: Spirituality & Education	7.95	
	Cash Total Tapes		
	TOTAL TAPES & BOOKS		
	10% Handling & Shipping		
	TOTAL		

ALL MONIES MUST BE IN U.S. FUNDS ONLY
PAYABLE THROUGH A CONTINENTAL U.S. BANK

Check Money Order Visa Mastercard

NAME _____

STREET _____

CITY _____ STATE _____ ZIP ____

Card Number _____ Expires ____

Signature _____

MAIL YOUR ORDER TODAY TO: BEAR & COMPANY, INC. PO DRAWER 2860, SANTA FE, NEW MEXICO 87501

PHONE TODAY: 1-800-WE-BEARS

Bear and Company, Inc.

publishes a complete line of creation centered^{TM} spirituality materials by Matt Fox and associates.

+ Fine Books including: Whee! We, wee
  Western Spirituality
+ A "little magazine" : Bear & Company
+ Program materials including cassette tapes & spirit masters.

Order from your local bookstore. For the location of the store nearest you featuring Bear & Company or for a complete catalog please fill out this form or call (505) 983-5968.

To: BEAR AND COMPANY, INC.
Santa Fe, New Mexico 87504-2860

Send to: _____
Street _____
City/State _____Zip _____

☐ Please send me a catalog

☐ Put me on your mailing list

☐ Which store in my area carries Bear & Company materials

☐ I am interested in your "little Magazine"

☐ I am interested in program materials